PUSHKIN PRESS

Bir

'I tend my herd and flock b   t; I cannot put it down'

Rosamund Young, author of *The Secret of Life of Cows*

'A convincing account of total dedication and self-belief, and there's beauty and joy in Len's strange life... entertaining and thought-provoking'

Guardian

'Truly original... There's a sense of birdlike lightness and agility about this episodic, elliptical novel'

Daily Mail

'Fascinating and affecting, a portrait of a woman determined to follow her passion come what may'

European Literature Network

'In this perfect match of writer and subject, Eva Meijer brilliantly evokes the precious, vibrant and complex society Len Howard shared with songbirds at her cottage in Sussex'

Sue Donaldson, author of *Zoopolis*

'Mesmerising and moving'

NRC Handelsblad

'You totally identify with Howard, making her passion your own. It isn't Howard who is eccentric, but people who live without birds'

Tzum

'Read this book to totally unwind. It will open your eyes and encourage you to go out and see the birds'

De Wereld Draait Door

'An eye-opening novel. What makes *Bird Cottage* so appealing is the quiet serenity that Eva Meijer displays'

De Volkskrant

EVA MEIJER is an author, artist, singer, songwriter and philosopher. *Bird Cottage* was nominated for the BNG and Libris prizes in the Netherlands and is being translated into six languages. Her non-fiction study on animal communication, *Animal Languages*, is out in 2019, and *The Limits of my Language* is forthcoming from Pushkin Press.

BIRD COTTAGE

Translated by
Antoinette Fawcett

Eva Meijer

PUSHKIN PRESS

Pushkin Press
71–75 Shelton Street
London, WC2H 9JQ

Original text © Eva Meijer 2016
English translation © Antoinette Fawcett 2018

Bird Cottage was first published as *Het Vogelhuis*
by Uitgeverij Cossee, Amsterdam, 2016

First published by Pushkin Press in 2018
This edition first published in 2019

**N ederlands
letterenfonds
dutch foundation
for literature**

This publication has been made possible with
financial support from the Dutch Foundation for Literature

1 3 5 7 9 8 6 4 2

ISBN 13: 978 1 78227 395 0

Designed and typeset by Tetragon, London
Printed and bound by CPI Group (UK) Ltd, Croydon CRO 4YY

www.pushkinpress.com

Contents

PROLOGUE

1965

Jacob flies swiftly into the house, calls to me, and then immediately flies out again. He rarely makes a fuss about things, and never flies very far from the nest once his babies have hatched. He usually visits the bird table a few times in the morning, and then stays close to the wooden nesting box on the birch tree. He is a placid bird, large for a Great Tit, and a good father.

I follow him out of doors and hear the machine even before I've left the garden. I run clumsily on clogs that almost slip off my feet. No. This can't be happening. Not that hedge. Not in the springtime. But a stocky man is trimming the hedge with one of those electric hedge-cutter things. He can't hear me through the racket. I squeeze between the hedge and the machine. The noise drowns out everything, crashing in waves over me, boring through my body.

It gives him a shock to see me there, suddenly in front of him. He switches the thing off and removes his ear-protectors. "What's up, missus?"

"You mustn't trim this hedge. It's full of nests. Most of the eggs have already hatched." My voice is shriller than usual. It feels as if someone is strangling me.

"You'll have to speak to the Council about it." He turns the machine on again.

No. Twigs jab at my back. I move to the left when he moves, and then to the right.

"Get out of my way, please."

"If you want to trim this hedge, you'll have to get rid of me first."

He sighs. "I'll start work on the other side, then." He holds the contraption at the ready, more as a shield than a weapon.

But that's where the Thrushes are, with their brown-speckled breasts. I shake my head. "No. You really mustn't."

"Look, missus, I'm just doing my job."

"What is your boss's phone number?"

He gives me a name and the County Council number. I keep an eye on him until he has left the lane. He's probably off to another hedge now.

Cheeping and chirping everywhere. The parent birds are nowhere to be seen, but the babies make their presence known. The parents will return and with any luck they won't have had too great a shock. I hurry to the house, sweat running down my back. I don't even pause to take off my cardigan.

"May I speak to Mr Everitt, please? It's urgent."

While I'm waiting for him, Terra comes and perches beside me. She can always tell when something is wrong. Birds are much more sensitive than we are. I'm still panting a little.

"Mr Everitt, I appreciate your coming to the telephone. Len Howard speaking, from Ditchling. This morning I discovered, to my great horror, that one of your workmen was trimming the hedges. It's the nesting season! I'm making a study of these birds. My research will be ruined."

Mr Everitt says I have to send in a written request to have the hedge-cutting postponed so that the Council can decide on the matter. He can't make that decision himself. I thank him very much and ask for a guarantee that there'll be no further hedge-trimming till then.

"I'll try my best," he says. "They do usually listen to me." He coughs, like a smoker.

I know the Great Tits would immediately warn me if they came back to trim the hedges, but for the rest of the day I feel very agitated. Sometimes the wind sounds like hedge-trimming; sometimes I'm tricked by a car in the distance. Jacob also remains restless. And that's not like him at all. He's old enough—at least six—to know better.

I start writing my letter. They must listen to me.

* * *

Early the next morning I make a trip into the village. It is the first really warm day of the year. The air seems to press me down, deeper into the road. My body is too heavy really, always getting heavier. In the past it used to take me ten minutes to walk there, but now the journey takes almost twenty. I rap on the grocer's window. It isn't nine o'clock yet. "Theo?" I knock again and spot his tousled white head of hair moving behind the counter. He stands up and raises his hand. In greeting? Or as a signal for me to wait a while?

Rummaging noises, the sound of metal on metal.

"Gwendolen! What brings you here so early?" Sleep still lingers in his face, tracing lines as fine as spider silk.

I tell him that the Council is planning to have the hedge trimmed and show him my letter. "Will you sign it too?"

He puts on his spectacles, carefully reads what I've written, then searches in three different drawers for a pen. "Esther was serving in the shop yesterday. Everything's in a muddle. A moment ago I couldn't find the key to the front door."

"How is Esther?"

"She's saving up for a scooter. Her parents aren't at all keen, but all the lasses have one." He looks at me over the top of his spectacles and gives a brief shrug.

"Is she sixteen already? Goodness!" I still have the image of her as a little girl, his daughter's first daughter. A precocious child, with eyes that seemed like openings to another world. Her eyes are still like that, heavily accentuated with kohl.

"Not yet. Next month. Why don't you leave the letter here, Gwen? Then I can ask all my customers to sign it."

"Good idea." We agree that I'll return for it later in the day. I thank him, pick up my shopping basket, and begin my usual rounds. The baker gives me one of yesterday's loaves. The butcher has saved some offcuts of bacon. The green-grocer presents me with a bag of old apples. I had thought of going to Brighton today, to the tree nursery, but I decided against it. It's far too hot to tackle those steep streets. On the way home Jacob comes to say hallo, and I catch sight of the pair of Robins who nested in my garden last year. Perhaps they're nesting in my neighbour's garden this year, which would not be very clever. Her cat is a terrible bird-hunter, the worst I know, even worse than the little black cat she had before. Moreover, this cat is very curious and peeks in all the nest boxes, which means that every cat in the neighbourhood knows where they are. I've told my neighbour three times now that she is responsible for all the consequent tragedies.

The Great Tits are sunning themselves in the front garden, their wings outspread. Jacob and Monocle II are sitting next to each other, very fraternally, as if they don't usually spend the whole day quarrelling. It's the heat that has made them so placid. Terra is on the path. She has positioned herself exactly where I always walk. Jacob's oldest son is perched on a low, broad branch. He is a little slower than the others—too much feeding at my bird table! Inside, I flop down onto the spindle-backed chair. I'll have to make the whole journey again soon. Cutie lands on my hair, then immediately flies up, and here comes Buffer. It's a game the baby birds discover anew, every year. They fly from the cupboard to my head, from my head to the table, from the table to the cupboard, three rapid rounds, then wing their way out of the window, so swift and full of now, only now.

*   *   *

At the top of the path Jacob comes to warn me. Even before hearing the noises, I know they're at it again. Since I received the letter from the Council—apologies, absolutely impossible, merely private concerns, important planning considerations—and sent them my objections, I have barely been away from here for almost a fortnight. Yesterday I received a message that the mayor is considering my objections after all, so I thought the danger was over. I walk as swiftly as I can, lame as an old horse. There are three of them this time. Jacob is flying madly back and forth, and so are all the other Great Tits, and the Robins, and the pair of Sparrows.

"There are nests in that hedge," I cry out, my heart thudding in my throat. But it's already happened, only the Blackbirds left, perhaps they've fledged already, but the baby Robins were still too little.

A carrot-headed young fellow, with collar-length hair and a round, freckled face, takes off his ear-protectors. "'Scuse me?"

"You've killed all the baby birds." I spurt the words out, spraying spittle with them.

He looks at the hedge, eyes squeezed tight against the sun, holds his breath a moment, hesitates. "Sorry."

"See what you've done now." Jacob is crying out and complaining. The Sparrows are cheeping, calling to the other Sparrows. The Blackbirds are making a terrible crying sound that I've never heard from them before.

The young fellow gazes at the Thrushes and the Robins and the Titmice flying back and forth over the hedge, to the field and back again, over the heads of his co-workers, towards me. A cloud passes over his blue eyes. He stops the other two men and points at the Sparrows just across from him. They fall silent and I can hear the birds cry out even louder. They're calling and calling, exactly as they do when Magpies attack their nests, but this time they don't stop.

I stay where I am until the men are out of sight. All the birds have deserted the hedge. Only Jacob remains. I call him, offer a peanut. He doesn't come.

I walk along the hedge looking for nests, to see if there are any babies left behind. I can't see anyone any more, just little feathers caught among the cut leaves and twigs. At the corner I find a little one that has fallen from its nest. It's a Sparrow, newly fledged. I carefully lift up the little brown body, already knowing that things aren't right. The creature trembles and then goes totally still, stiller than any stillness that holds life. With my other hand I make a little hollow in the earth beneath the hedge, lay him gently down, then cover him up.

The silence wraps itself round me, accompanies me home, where the Great Tits are flying around more nervously than normal. I put food on the bird table for them, earlier than I usually do. Perhaps this will distract them—peanuts, bread, some pieces of pear, but nothing fatty because it's the nesting season.

This late springtime green is still overwhelming, still so brilliant—a luxuriant abundance. I sit down on one of the old garden chairs by the front of the house. My hip seems to want to work itself free from my body. This damned old body.

Terra lands on my shoulder. Her tiny claws prick into the fabric of my blouse. She is so dependent on me, even though she never sleeps indoors. She made her nest in the tall apple tree, thank goodness, not in the hedge. The hedge-cutting didn't make much of an impression on her—she has enough experience to know that it's not worth getting too excited. She taps her beak against my shoulder, very lightly, as if she's trying to remind me of something.

STAR 1

Behaviourism, the theory that dominates all contemporary research into animal behaviour, assumes that scientifically valid data can only be obtained in situations free from extraneous stimuli, in which reactions can be measured in reproducible experiments. The animal mind, which includes the human mind, is viewed as being a kind of black box into which we have no access. From this standpoint, the description of natural behaviour adds little to scientific knowledge since such behaviour cannot objectively be measured. Darwin's work on animal intelligence, for example, is regarded as unscientific because it is primarily based on anecdotal evidence. Behaviourism, however, does not properly take account of the fact that many animals behave differently in captivity than when they are free. Most birds are timid by nature, actually often afraid of human beings, and when they are kept in laboratories their behaviour and the research results are bound to be affected. Furthermore, any empirical research based on the notion that the thoughts and feelings of animals are unknowable can only produce results that support this picture. If you perceive someone as a machine, then your research questions will reflect that, and will determine the space in which the object of your enquiry can respond. Note well, I have deliberately used the word "object" here. The so-called objective method of studying animals is, therefore, just as coloured by assumptions as any other.

It is now well over ten years since I moved to the little house in Sussex that I would later call Bird Cottage. It is situated on the edge of a small wood and is close to an area of great natural beauty where countless birds and other creatures live: Wood Pigeons and Cuckoos, Foxes and Badgers,

Field Mice and Moles, Buzzards and Tawny Owls, Chiffchaffs and Pochards. In the trees and bushes surrounding the house there are also a great number of small birds, such as Blackbirds, Great Tits, Robins and Sparrows. Soon after moving in I set up a bird table on the terrace in front of the cottage, and at seven o'clock each morning and at five in the afternoon I would put out all kinds of titbits for them. I also placed a bird bath there and hung up a few nest boxes: on the house itself, the old oak and the apple tree. It did not take long for the first inquisitive Titmice to come and investigate. The Sparrows immediately chased them off. They will take over any territory if they have the chance. But the Sparrows were more afraid of me than the Tits were, and because I spent a great deal of time observing the birds from the garden bench, all of them had the opportunity to eat the food on the table, and all could inspect the changes that were happening in the house.

I came to live here in February 1938. Most of the birds were already busy looking for places to build their nests and, in some cases, for a suitable mate. They were more interested in each other than in me. In March, however, that began to change. One of the Great Tits, Billy, an older male with a proud bearing and a loud voice, was cheekier than the rest. He was the first to fly each morning to the bird table and every afternoon he would visit the bird bath for an elaborate wash. One warm day in April he flew through the open window and into the house. He fluttered around the sitting room and then rushed swiftly out of the window again. The next day he came once more. One of the ways that Great Tits learn is by watching each other closely, and before very long Billy's partner, Greenie, came inside with him too. I called her Greenie because of the green sheen on her feathers. From then on I always left the top light of the window open so they could fly in and out as they pleased. This was the start of a very special way of living that has continued to this very day, and has taught me a great deal.

1900

"Look, Lennie." Papa is holding something in his hands. I run towards him.

"Is it a Titmouse, Papa?"

"It's a Blue Tit. He's fallen from his nest. I found him under one of the beech trees, by the girls' school. Or rather, Peter found him." Peter wags his tail at the sound of his name. "Now, you keep hold of him for a moment, and I'll find a box to put him in."

Its little feathers! I've never felt anything so soft in all my life. I shape my hands into a little bowl, a small nest, and lift them to my mouth. I give the birdie a light kiss. So soft! So blue, that tiny head! The creature stirs, shivers a little. It startles me, but I hold my hands firmly together.

"Put him in here. Very carefully." Papa has brought a cardboard box from his study, with an old scarf lining the bottom.

I gently lower my cupped hands till they touch the bottom of the box, then slowly pull them apart.

"Well done. And now we'll go and buy him some food." He takes me by the hand. Olive and Kings and Duddie all go to school and Mama won't let me go there yet, but now I'm in luck. At last, I'm the lucky one!

"Flossie?" Papa pops his head round the door into my mother's bedroom. "I'm just taking Lennie into town to buy some mince for the Blue Tit."

"Please call her Gwendolen, her proper name. And shouldn't you be working?" My mother's voice sounds lighter than it has done these past few days. Perhaps she doesn't have a headache any more.

Papa turns a deaf ear to her objections.

"Come here, Gwendolen." Reluctantly, I enter the dark room. It smells of sleep and of something else too. Something old. My mother adjusts my dress and presses me against her. She is the source of the smell. When she releases me, I quickly run back to my father, who is waiting outside.

I skip along the broad pavement, in exact time with Papa's footsteps. "Where are we going?"

"First to the butcher's, and then to Mr Volt's."

I prance along, raising my legs higher and higher. I'm very good at it. My feet touch the ground at precisely the same point as Papa's. Pa-dum, pa-dum. The hooves of a half-horse.

When we reach the butcher's, Peter has to wait outside. He sits down immediately. He knows what he has to do. I stroke his white bib a moment, then quickly follow Papa into the shop.

"Some finely minced beef, please. It's for a Blue Tit, so don't give me too much." Fat Jimmy doesn't always serve in the shop, only if Mr Johnson, the butcher, isn't there. He's very slow and he doesn't give me a slice of ham.

"Thank you. And may I also have a slice of ham, please?"

Fat Jimmy shrugs his shoulders and turns to slice the ham. My father gives me a wink. When we're outside again, he tears the slice of ham in two. One half for Peter and one for me.

Mr Volt sells everything. One of his eyes droops a little lower than the other, and it bulges too. Duddie says someone once gave him a great thump and his eye flew out of his head and then it didn't want to go back in again, and Olive says he can't see out of it any more, but he always looks at me with it, as if he really can see me like that, as if he actually can see more with that eye than other people, things they can't see.

"Good day, Mr Howard. Good day, young lady. What can I do for you both?"

"Some birdseed, please. For a little Blue Tit."

"Certainly, sir. Our Universal Blend. How much would you like?" He takes down a canister from the topmost shelf, and picks up a paper bag.

"Just enough till the little one can fly again," Papa says.

The whole shop is full of canisters and storage bins and in the corner there's a skeleton. I walk towards it, finger the bones, and then shrink back when the skeleton starts moving.

"Oh, dearie me," says Mr Volt. "Be careful now. Sometimes the spirit suddenly moves him."

"How much do I owe you?" Papa asks.

"Oh, it's hardly worth adding to your account, sir. Now then, young lady."

I go to the counter.

"A bull's eye or a humbug?"

"A humming bug, please!"

From one of the glass jars that are kept behind the counter, he takes out a sweetie. It's green and red and looks like a stripy beetle.

"Thank you!" I curtsey to him, just like I've practised with Olive.

"What lovely manners!"

Peter races home ahead of us. The humbug melts in my mouth and it's very sweet. I take it out to see if it still looks like a beetle. But the bug has become a flat patch. Paddy the Patch Bug.

Tessa opens the door for us, at the precise moment that we arrive. I run past her through the high-ceilinged entrance hall and into the parlour, where the box with the Blue Tit is still on the table.

"He's still alive!"

"That's good. So now we can get to work. What's the time?"

I go and take a look at the clock on the windowsill. "It's three o'clock."

"Exactly three o'clock?"

"Almost exactly. One minute past, no, two minutes past three."

"Yes, that's almost exactly. Now listen. We must feed the birdie once an hour." He forms some of the minced meat into a tiny ball and pushes it into the bird's throat with his little finger. The bird swallows, and I give a very soft cheer.

"Soon I'll mix the birdseed and the minced meat together, with a little water. And then it's just a question of feeding him. If the birdie lives till tomorrow, you can feed him too." He gives the Blue Tit another little ball of food, and then another, till the birdie doesn't want any more. My father's fingers are long and clever. I watch everything he does very closely, so that tomorrow I can do it too.

"Go and ask Cook if she has a foot stove. I have the impression that this little chap is cold."

"Can't I hold him?"

My father shakes his head. I run to the kitchen.

"Cook, Cook, we've got a little Blue Tit! And he's cold! Do you perhaps have a foot stove for him?"

I hop from my left foot to my right foot, from my right foot to my left.

"Goodness gracious, child, calm down!"

Cook slowly gets out of her chair and stands up, groaning.

"Come on then, but no more shouting. Your mother isn't well."

I follow her down the steep, narrow staircase into the cellar. Small footsteps, my hand against the clammy wall.

"If he's still alive tomorrow, then I'm allowed to feed him."

Cook hums a little, then finds a foot stove in the open cupboard by the back wall. I take it from her.

"Tread carefully," she calls after me, but I'm nearly upstairs already.

STAR 2

Countless numbers of Tits, Blackbirds, Sparrows and Robins lived in and around the garden of Bird Cottage. And there were also regular visitors, such as Jackdaws, Crows, Jays, Blue Tits, Finches and Woodpeckers. Some birds, such as the Swallows, returned every year; others visited now and then. There were birds who should have been summer visitors, but who stayed in the neighbourhood for their whole lives; others came for a season, or a number of years. Nearly every kind of bird has taken a peek inside the cottage at some point, but I have always tried to keep birds of the Crow family outside, as much as possible. They upset the smaller birds and rob their nests. The birds with whom I have developed the closest bond are the Great Tits. Great Tits are perhaps the cleverest birds of all, and full of curiosity. They are ideal research partners.

During their first visits Billy and Greenie were clearly quite nervous still, but very soon they began to stay inside, especially when the autumn gave way to a winter with several weeks of snow. Other Great Tits soon followed their example, and that December the first ones began to search for roosts in the house. Their choices were not always happy—they would roost between the curtain rods and the ceiling, or in the frame of a sliding door, which meant that it could no longer be closed—and so I began to hang boxes on the walls, or old food cartons, or small wooden cases. Each time they swiftly understood their purpose and it was not long before several different Great Tits had taken possession of a roosting box of their own. They squabbled less about their roosts when they were inside than they did out of doors, perhaps because they viewed the cottage as my territory. In the breeding season, however, they always looked for an outdoor spot where they could nest. Up to now, not one Tit has nested inside the house. Perhaps, after all, there is insufficient privacy here.

The Great Tits soon grew to know me, and although my presence sometimes influenced their behaviour (they would startle, for example, if I suddenly stood up; and when I was coming in I had to sing out "Peanut!" from behind the door, to tell them I was entering), most of the time they carried on as usual. Not only did that give me the opportunity to study their behaviour, I was also able to record their interrelationships from close at hand. In this way I became acquainted with around forty different Great Tits, all of whom had their own particular inclinations and wishes.

I learned from the birds themselves that individual intelligence plays a much greater role in their behaviour and choices than biologically determined tendencies, or "instinct", as scientists call it. In order to study the birds like this, it was important to keep other human beings away from the cottage as much as possible. Birds react to the tiniest change in vocal inflection and to the smallest disturbance in their environment. Even visitors who did their best to make no noise often behaved in such a way that the birds would simply wish to escape as swiftly as possible. Once birds have had a shock it takes a long time for them to return—at least half a day, for the most part.

In my interactions with the Great Tits I have often felt myself to be slow and clumsy. Great Tits have better hearing than humans and a wider field of vision. Their eyes are on the sides of their heads and their vision is partly monocular (seeing differently with each eye) and partly binocular (with two eyes at the same time). This gives them a very wide range indeed. Their powers of observation are far sharper than those of humans. They are much more sensitive, not only to disturbances in their environment, but also to changes in the weather, to the colour of fruit and especially of berries, and to the movements of other creatures. There are, of course, many similarities too. Just like people, they are creatures of habit. Like us they have fixed rituals, when eating or going to sleep, for example. There are always around six or seven Great Tits sleeping in roosting boxes inside the house. Some birds only come indoors when it is really cold, but others will sleep in a box fixed to the picture rail below the bedroom ceiling for most of the year.

Like us, birds have countless ways of communicating with each other: through calls and songs, posture, the sound their wings make, eye contact, touching, movements, little dances. My interactions with the Great Tits soon became just as rich and varied. I regularly spoke to them. They would intuitively know from the tone of my voice what I intended, and in the course of time they learned the meaning of the words I used. They understood my gestures and we would make eye contact with each other. Some of the birds even enjoyed perching near me or on me.

Birds always see me quicker than I see them. When I turn my face towards them, they have already turned to me. And it is not only that they see me quicker because their eyes are set on the sides of their heads; it is also because they move more swiftly. At first I had the feeling that they understood me better than I understood them, but later I could read them just as well as they could read me. I understood some individuals better than others, of course, just as is the case with people. A few birds were really special: Baldhead, for example, the male Great Tit, who in the last days of his life was so tame that he lay in my lap all day long. And there was Twist, a brave and very intelligent female, who was my first guide in the language of Great Tits. And Star, of course, the cleverest Great Tit I have been privileged to know, and the one with whom I developed the closest ties.

1911

It feels as if someone has opened a door into my heart so the warmth can stream in. A little door, or a window perhaps. I run towards Olive, at the bottom of the garden, through the summer grass, the soft grass. Everything is so green.

"Is Father there yet?" she asks.

I shake my head. "Have you smelled the roses? Look, they're in full bloom now." I clasp hold of a rose in the hedge behind her and bend it down to her.

She nods, then stretches her back. "Would you be a darling and fetch me a drink? I've been on my feet all day." She had to spend the day with Mother, shopping for dresses.

I walk back to the house, more slowly now, step by step by step. Mother stops me in the conservatory. "Gwen, are you ready for the performance? Your father will be down in less than half an hour. He'll recite some of his latest poems, then Paul will read one of his sequences, and then you perhaps could play that Bach suite for us."

I shrug my shoulders.

"Gwendolen." She gives me a stern look.

"Yes, Mother." I carry on to the kitchen, where I ask Tessa if I may have a glass of champagne, "For my sister."

"And how are the birdies, miss?"

"The baby Great Tit didn't survive. But yesterday I let the Magpie fly away. That seems to be going well."

"You're a real angel, miss. I was just saying that to Cook."

I wave goodbye and take the champagne out. Paul is leaning against the doorpost, his curls making little circles on the wall, his face turned to the low evening sun. As I pass him, he turns towards me. I jump, blush, pretend I haven't seen him.

"Gwendolen?"

I look back.

"Is that really wise, before your performance?"

"It's for Olive." My fingers firmly clasp the glass. I mustn't grasp it too tightly, otherwise it will shatter. And I mustn't let go.

"I know. I was just teasing."

I blush even more now.

"I'm looking forward to hearing you play."

I nod and swiftly walk on. The champagne is splashing over the brim of the glass and onto my fingers. I should have said something about his poems, that my father let me read them, and that they're alive, they fly, they move me.

"Thanks." Olive has put the parasol up, even though she is sitting in the shade. "Are you about to start?"

"Papa will be there soon. In half an hour."

From the corner of my eye I can see Paul diminishing, a doll in evening dress, a little man on a bridal cake. My cousin Margie speaks of marriage as if it were a form of imprisonment.

"Will you play the Bach Cello Suite?"

I nod in agreement, running through the notes in my head.

"Is Stockdale here?"

"He's supposed to be coming." I hope he does. Stockdale conducts a London orchestra and it's a while since he last heard me play. I've improved. I've studied very hard these past few months.

Charles, the Crow that Papa raised, flies into the ivy. He hops onto my outstretched hand, then back onto a branch. He doesn't like all this commotion. He flies off and as he does so poops on the rim of Mr Wayne's glass, who only spots it as he takes a sip of his champagne. Wayne teaches music in Towyn.

"That vile man." Olive pulls a face.

Last time Stockdale was here he made eyes at Margie, rather conspicuously, I thought. She's twenty-two years old and is studying at the Slade School of Art. She's staying with us this summer because her parents are travelling. Margie flirts with everyone and they all put up with it because she seems so innocent. Stockdale clearly thought he'd hooked her, until at the end of the evening Margie began to yawn terribly and excused herself, giving a little wave at us from the staircase before vanishing.

Olive takes the bowl of nuts from the table and puts it on the edge of her chair. She picks out the tastiest, popping them into her mouth, one after another.

Tessa comes to fetch us. It's warm inside, a throng of people, bodies that leave hardly any space, words that barely or don't reach their targets. Words that simply express habit, that hardly mean anything else at all.

People travel far for these soirées. My father is the only one in this part of Wales to organise such evenings on a regular basis. Stockdale presses my hand. A little too long. He breathes out so heavily that the carnation in his button-hole trembles.

My mother is standing by the grand piano. "I'd like to welcome all of you." She speaks differently on these evenings, more affectedly.

I can see the broad, blond head of my brother Dudley on the other side of the room, and I move towards him, as inconspicuously as possible.

"I can wait." My mother lifts an eyebrow. People are laughing. Dudley shifts along to make room for me.

Paul is sitting almost behind me. I become aware of how my back looks in this rose-coloured gown, chosen for me by Mother: too womanly, too close-fitting. My mother announces his name first and then mine, as if we belong together, as if our names follow each other's by force of logic.

Newman, my father, starts with the second poem from his book *Footsteps of Proserpine*. It's all about love and Blackbirds. Many of the poems in this collection were written for Mother. I suppress a yawn and move my fingers a little to warm them up. Ta-dada-da-dadada. He recites two more poems from his first collection, then declaims a long one about a city, which time has so much altered, and then another about the Trojan War, from his Greek cycle. His poems, without exception, are far too long and contain too many adjectives. Before Papa became a poet he was an accountant.

Kingsley, my oldest brother, rushes in panting and drops down so hard onto a chair in the back row that everyone turns around. He is still wearing flannels and I can smell him even from where I am seated. When I look at him, he pulls a funny face.

My father's voice goes up a tone. He lets one more pause fall, then ends on a note of triumph. Paul walks to the front during the applause and I look at his feet, then briefly at his face, with the sun in it. My eyes fleetingly meet his. He is already speaking. I hardly hear what he says, but I know the words. And then it's over.

My mother introduces me. I tune up. My fingers are tingling. And then I play: a question, an answer, a question.

*   *   *

When everyone has left, I come downstairs again. I go to where he stood, six feet away from where I was sitting, perhaps eight feet or so. I can see myself perched there, glancing sideways, turning my head. My cheeks are on fire again. Through the window I see my father pouring champagne into a glass. He gives it to my mother. The house is clearly breathing once again, through the open windows, while the last light of day dies away.

When I'd finished playing, Paul came to talk to me. He asked if I intended to take my musical ambitions further. I shrugged. "Possibly."

"Then you must move to London."

"I realise that."

"I have acquaintances there. I could help you find lodgings."

I nodded, thanked him, then said: "Sorry, but my mother wants to talk to me." My mother! I'm almost eighteen.

"Of course." He gave a nod and walked away. I took a deep breath, breathed in, breathed out. Outside the air smelled of grass and fire, of perfume. I thought he'd follow me, otherwise I'd still be speaking to him now. Expectations adhere to each other, forming even greater expectations. Something insignificant is added to the heap, and then something else, until it's hard to see over the top, and then it's difficult not to perceive yourself as hemmed in, and then it's difficult to tell the difference between what is and what might be. Until he has gone, that is. Perhaps it will be weeks until I see him again. I should have said something smart or witty. The sun inside my breast departs, leaving a question mark in its place, an imprint of yearning. I could simply have talked to him a while. He wouldn't have said what he did without a reason, those things about lodgings and acquaintances and so on. And he recited his poem about the woman who is always searching.

My father beckons me. I go outside.

"You played beautifully, my darling." He hiccups, puts his arm around me, draws me towards him. The wind brings the smell of the sea with it, not the salt.

My mother drains her glass in one swift draught.

I wriggle free. "I want to study at the College of Music."

"Sweetheart, you're much too young still." My father smiles apologetically at me.

"And then you'd have to move to London," my mother says. "My little girl. I'm not sure you could cope." She touches my cheek, gives it a little pinch.

"Of course I'll cope."

She is silent. My father stares into the dark garden.

"Of course I'll cope," I repeat, more loudly. "I'm not a child any more."

My father puts his hand on my shoulder. I shake it off. Inside the house my shoes leave earth behind them, and grass.

I meet my sister on the staircase, holding a plate with a sandwich in her hand. "Weren't they charming?" she says. "Paul's poems, I mean."

"I think I love him," I say.

"You're *in* love, and that's a completely different matter." She looks at me sternly. "You mustn't confuse one feeling with another, you know." According to her it would be better not to act on feelings at all.

I heave a deep sigh.

"Stop acting all romantic." She follows me into my room, sits on the bed and starts eating. She hardly eats at all during dinner and then afterwards she's always hungry. "You really did play beautifully though."

"I want to be a violin player. To play every evening. To build a new life, in London or somewhere else. I want to earn my own living." I must find out what's involved in taking the entrance examination for the College of Music, when I can do it, what my standard has to be.

"You don't need to earn a living, surely? We're rich enough."

"I want to lead my own life."

"You can do that here too, can't you?"

I shake my head.

She puts the plate with its half-eaten sandwich on my bedside table and says good night.

I walk to the window. My parents are outside still, sitting on the bench. There is a little table in front of them with two glasses, an ashtray and my father's book of poems. I can't hear the Blackbird any more. I shut the curtains and undress myself. When I take off my dress, I can smell myself in the fabric. Myself and this evening. The imprint of the waistband remains on my skin. I fetch my diary and sit down.

Charles visited the garden this morning and came again in the evening. After everyone had left, though, I didn't see him any more. He has probably gone to his roosting place at the edge of the wood. The Blackbird I heard must have been Mike, who has been living in our garden this past week. For a number of years now I have kept a record of all the birds who visit our garden, and sometimes I write stories about them. Papa is the only one who thinks they're any good. Last year I sent a few of them to a magazine, but they didn't give me an answer. So it's better for me to focus on music. But birds are important for composers too. Paul told me, not so long ago, that Mozart was inspired by his pet Starlings. Paul. I write his name down, then scribble it out again.

Longing is—

Understanding that you are fathomless.

Understanding that you are flux.

Understanding that you are water and that water cannot be grasped.

*   *   *

The light in the old school seems tangible. Dust lends substance to the sunbeams. My nose is itching.

"Just a few more moments," Margie says, impatiently holding her hand up. "I've almost got you."

I give my nose a scratch.

"Come on, Gwen. Lie still a moment, won't you?"

I gaze at the tear in the wallpaper behind her. The school closed a few years back and the building is no longer in use. Three weeks ago Margaret found out that the back door, half overgrown with ivy, is not actually locked.

"We can go in," she announced yesterday evening. "Otherwise they'd have made sure the door was properly closed."

She has placed me on a table and draped a sheet around my body. Charles came with us, but after a quarter of an hour he flew out again. Not enough action. And nothing to eat.

"Yes. That's good now. I'm sorry, darling, I really do appreciate your posing for me. I know it's hot." She takes a step back, squeezes her eyes half-shut.

The tear in the wallpaper becomes a person, an animal, a patch.

"Ladies." His voice.

"Paul!" Margaret says. "What are you doing here?"

"Your uncle asked me to come and fetch you. Hallo, Gwen. You're looking quite, um, extraordinary."

"I'm not allowed to move," I reply. "Talking counts as moving."

Paul says they're going sailing and we have to come along.

"Art First," Margaret says. "I need a little longer. When are you setting off?"

Has he come here because of me? I keep still, watch how they're talking to each other. He clearly isn't seeing me any more, yet now he's looking at the painting and then for an instant, probingly, at me.

"We set off in fifteen minutes," he answers.

"Then you must leave at once," Margaret tells him. She straightens her checked skirt.

He looks at me again before he leaves the room, as if there's something in me to be discovered. I can sense the palms of my hands, the soles of my feet, my skin in places that are otherwise silent.

Margaret lays a few more brushstrokes, but the visit has distracted her, it seems. "We should go really, don't you think?"

"I don't particularly want to go sailing."

"Well, I believe I'm ready." With the little finger of her right hand she wipes away some of the paint. I sit up. My feet have gone to sleep. I pull my dress on again, over my head.

"What do you think?" She turns the painting towards me.

I see a kind of goddess, or someone from another era, someone who has my face but is more beautiful, someone with a longer and more elegant body. There's a Crow in the corner of the painting, sitting on a pillar.

"You've invented that bosom," I say. I understand now why Paul was looking at me like that.

She smiles. "Your spitting image, right?"

"What will you do with it?"

"Oh, exhibit it, of course. Perhaps here, at the end of the season. It's perfect here." She leaves the room ahead of me, letting the canvas stay where it is. From a distance I can see that she has painted a window behind me, looking out on the sea.

*   *   *

"Lennie! Margie!" My father waves at us from the front of the boat.

I take his outstretched hand and step onto the deck. I walk to the stern, wood on water. I tug the fabric of my dress forward, then let it fall back against my skin. And again. Coolness.

Dudley is smoking, his long limbs stretched out on the bench. He rolls his eyes as I get closer: "Kingsley didn't want to join us. Playing tennis." Kingsley has played tennis every day this summer. Not once has he gone bird-watching with me.

Margaret shifts Dudley aside and sits down next to him. "Wonderful! Sailing in this weather." She stretches out her long legs and closes her eyes against the sun.

"Good to see you, ladies. And now we're just waiting for Paul and Dimitri." Mother is wearing her large tinted sunglasses and the dress everyone says makes her look so young. A sister to her daughters, not their mother. "Cook has made sandwiches for us," she says.

I walk to the boat rail, towards the hills in the distance.

"Ship ahoy!" Paul is standing on the quayside, bathed in light. Dimitri appears behind him. He's a poet too and one of Paul's friends. He sports a little moustache, twisted up at the ends with brilliantine. He is the son of Mr McWest, and McWest is a millionaire who spends the summer on his estate just outside Aberdovey. He's had his eye on Olive for a while now, but in her opinion he's a mere ne'er-do-well. "We've brought apples. And guitars!"

They dash down the stone steps and leap from the jetty onto the boat. My father pushes the boat off with an exaggerated flourish. We sail towards the hills, past banks of silt, near the castellated folly on the rock with the pine trees. The flag in front of the building is drooping. I go and sit on the foredeck with Father. When we were here last week we saw Peewits.

"When can we go to Ynys-hir again?" Father and I have gone bird-watching together these past few summers, on day trips to the salt marshes further up the coast.

"Darling, you're too old for that now. It's high time you started to behave like a young lady," my mother says, pulling my skirt straight.

"I didn't ask you," I say, shaking her hand off, shifting away from her.

"Hallo, Gwen." Dimitri sits down beside me and gives me a hand damp with perspiration. "Beautiful performance last week." He laughs a little. He has a high-pitched giggle with which he often ends his sentences. His milk-white legs are going to turn bright red in an instant.

"Thank you."

The rocks change from grey to white, yellowish on top.

"Paul said you were modelling. For Margaret. Are you an artist too?" His eyes blink against the light. His nervousness makes me nervous.

"I think I'll go and sit under the awning. I'm about to get sunburned." I stand up. "And no. I'm not an artist. No time for that lark."

"All right. So, now I know." He giggles again.

My father is talking to Paul, claps him on the shoulder. Dudley hangs over the rail, touching the water with his finger-tips. Olive is reading. My mother is looking for a glass in the picnic basket. My eyes meet Margaret's. The water swishes.

"Who'd like some lunch?" Mother is handing out the packed sandwiches.

Dimitri sits down beside Margaret. She starts to sketch him. He finds a pen and a notebook, shouts that he's going to write a poem about her, that she's a woman like a poem.

The bread is warm and soft, soggy, and the pieces of cucumber slide onto the napkin. I fish them up and wolf them down. I sense that Paul is looking at me.

"Delicious," my father says. "Delicious bread. I needed that." He pats his belly, which has greatly increased in size since he stopped work.

My mother gives him a disapproving look.

Paul comes and sits beside me. "How are your birds?" He tells me about a composer who works Blackbird song into his music.

"Olive, you must have a sandwich too." My mother tries to push it into Olive's hands, but my sister keeps them tightly closed.

"No, Mama. I'm dieting."

Mother isn't eating either. "Do you think it's time for a toast?" she asks.

Papa nods. "It's always time for a toast." He nods again. "And it's certainly the right time now."

Everyone stands up. Margaret and Dimitri put their things down and stand next to Dudley.

My father declaims his piece about the Trojan War and then says, "Cheers."

"Cheers," everyone replies, and then Dudley pushes Margaret over the boat rail, immediately leaping in after her. Dimitri and Paul shed their garments and dive in too.

"I think perhaps they shouldn't swim here," my father says, as he heaves the boat to. "The currents are treacherous."

My mother nods her head in agreement, because he has made a pronouncement. I very much doubt she could repeat what he said.

*   *   *

The tall grass tickles my legs. I walk on till I can no longer hear the others, squat behind a rhododendron bush and pull down my cotton knickers. I relieve myself, letting the stream flow between my feet. Too fiercely, it splashes against my calves. I hear something and swiftly pull up my knickers. Perhaps it was a rabbit in the distance, or a squirrel, perhaps only the wind rattling the twigs. I wipe my left calf against the calf of my right leg. The last drops have evaporated before I've even taken four steps.

Dimitri, Dudley and Olive are swimming. My parents are sitting on the picnic blanket.

I paddle into the water. I'd like to swim too, but I didn't bring a bathing costume with me.

"Where's Margaret?"

My father turns towards me. "No idea," he says, speaking slowly. His legs stand out, white against the sand.

"Papa, you're drunk."

"We're simply enjoying the summer, sweetheart." He doesn't see my irritation, picks up a guitar and bursts into song. No one joins in.

I walk up the hill, looking for Margaret. It seems to be getting hotter and hotter. My body feels heavier. Sand on sand.

I walk along a little path that leads to the wood, its shade drawing me towards it. After a short climb, I see a meadow on my left. Swallows are circling above, swooping down almost to grass level, tumbling over each other, downwards, upwards. I follow the blue flowers. A hare bolts off.

I hear them before I can see them. "Ow, ow. Something's stinging me."

"Yes, darling. You did want to be beside the pond. Water means midges."

I take another step, still hidden by the hill. I see them lying there, entwined, one body made from two, and then a leg moves, an arm. He's tickling her. She pretends she wants to break free.

I recoil, stumble, out of sight already. They must have heard me, but so what? I was looking for Margaret. They shouldn't have been so secretive. I refuse to walk quietly. There's a crack between my breasts, spreading down through my whole body: first a line, then an opening, then a gaping hole. The path blurs. I angrily wipe the tears away. Why didn't I know about this? Does everyone else know? Why couldn't I see it? Why does he look at me like that then? And Margaret—she knows what I feel. They must have been laughing at me.

I run past my parents at a brisk trot, so they won't notice my tears, pull my dress off when I reach the water, and jump in, clad only in my chemise, swimming underwater to the others. Dimitri whistles. Olive laughs. Dudley splashes water at me. I swim round the boat and imagine that the hole in my breast is filling with water. When I follow the others out of the river I feel as if I've turned to liquid. My mother looks at my chemise with distaste. My father's eyes are sleepy. Drops of water run down my legs, making little streams that flow back to the estuary.

"We should go back soon," my father says. "They're forecasting bad weather at the end of the day."

"Margie!" Dudley shouts at the top of his voice. "Paul!"

"Have they gone somewhere together then?" Olive says, frowning.

"Gwen, did you catch sight of them just now?" My mother takes off her sunglasses and throws a shawl round her shoulders.

I shake my head. A fist clenches in my stomach.

There comes Margaret, the filly, frisking back through the meadow, sketchbook in hand. "Are we leaving already? I was by a little pool. There were such beautiful butterflies there." She shows my mother her drawings, traces the butterflies with her fingers.

"So it's just Paul now."

At that moment Paul comes towards us from the other direction. His shirt is rumpled and there is sand in his hair. "Am I late? Sorry. I went to the woods to write something and fell asleep there."

Paul winks as he walks past me. I pretend not to notice and follow Olive to the fore-bench. She tells me about a book she was reading, where everything happens in a single day. Margaret joins my mother in the centre of the boat. "Are there any sandwiches left? I suddenly feel so hungry."

My mother slowly opens the picnic basket, lengthening the scene. This is her moment. Dudley suddenly also feels hungry, and Paul as well.

My father holds out his hand. "I'd like another one too."

"You've had enough already." My mother closes the picnic basket, smiling.

My father pulls it towards him. My mother keeps a tight grip on the handle. My father tugs harder. My mother presses her lips together. She grasps the handle more tightly still and it breaks away from the basket at one side. She loses her balance and falls backwards. The sandwiches slide out, landing in a neat row one behind the other.

"For the fishes," Margaret says, helping my mother to her feet again, and then she throws the sandwiches one by one into the water. Slices of cucumber are left on the bottom of the boat. My father sits down and stares intently at the horizon. Dudley and Paul steer the boat into the channel.

In the distance the clouds are piling higher, a dark-grey castle, and the only thing I long for is rain.

*   *   *

A rosy sun, rosy sky, blue sky, yellow sun. I'm lying in bed listening to Olive knock on the door, then my mother, then Olive again.

"Gwen?" she says, peeping her head round. "Are you all right?"

I sit up, my eyes feeling swollen. "I'm just a little unwell."

"Cook will make you some porridge. Shall I ask her to bring it to your bedroom?"

I shake my head. "I'll get up. Perhaps I ought to go out and get some fresh air."

"Are you sure you're all right? It's eleven o'clock already."

"Yes. Of course." I get out of bed, wash my face with water from the jug on the tall table in the corner. In the corridor I peer at my face in the looking glass. Dark spiky hair, a sharp nose, long cheeks, questioning eyes—I understand. I can't find anything attractive in my face either.

Dudley is lying like a beached seal, stretched out on the sofa. He's reading a book, *Jane Eyre*. My book.

"Good morning."

He turns a page with his fat fingers. His nails are rimmed with black. He does absolutely nothing at all. At least Kingsley works, at the factory owned by Dimitri's father.

"I said, good morning!" A door slams upstairs. "That's my book, by the way."

"Crikey, Gwen. Are you picking a quarrel?" He doesn't even look up as he says this.

I snatch the book from him, as if I'm eight instead of eighteen, as if he's ten instead of twenty.

"You're all so frightfully annoying." Limb by limb he begins to shift his body. "Mama?" he calls upstairs. "I'm going swimming."

Cook brings me the porridge. I eat it slowly, in small mouthfuls. When the plate is half empty, I take it to the kitchen. "Sorry," I say to Cook. "I don't feel very well."

I feel calmer once I'm outside. The heat makes me feel much better. "Charles, wait a minute." I could already see him from my window—he probably wants to go exploring with me. He waits in front of the house until I reach him, perched on the lowest branch of the oak tree. Then he darts up, flies off, flies back, far too frisky for this weather. The white rocks along the path feel warmer than usual and leave a chalkiness on my hand. My heart is beating much too fast. I slow down. The earth hums with heat. As I reach the first oak trees, I lose sight of Charles. He flew off down a side path and was flying too low for me to still see him. I choose the right path through sheer good luck. Something is rustling behind the fir trees—there's not a hint of a breeze, so it must be an animal, a rabbit probably. The path leads to a clearing. We've been here before, in the winter, when the woods were icy and sealed, the tree branches black and hard, the creatures hungry. In the shadow of a pool I see Charles. He solemnly wades into the water, left foot, right foot, his feathers puffed out against the heat. As he sinks down, the water ripples slowly away from him in circles. I take off my shoes. "Good idea, little one," I tell him.

Charles was only a few weeks old when my father found him. We thought he wouldn't survive. But after the first night I was allowed to keep him in my own room. At first he slept in a shoebox, then in a canary cage. He can't speak, but he understands a great deal and he's just like a dog. He loves following me everywhere and when he was younger he loved to play with sticks and balls. As soon as he could fly properly, I'd leave the window open for him, even when it was frosty, especially when it was frosty. At first, he'd come indoors every evening, but later he stayed away. Sometimes he flies with a group of other Crows, but I don't think he's found himself a mate. Perhaps he'll find someone next year, when they start nesting again in March.

The water is warmish by the edge of the pool, cooler where it gets deeper. Charles gives himself a shake, pecks at his feathers, stays in the shallows. Spatters of water pat onto the surface, clearly audible. We're the only ones here. The water makes my legs slanted and slender below the knee, makes my hands when I put them in more supple than usual. "I have to practise and practise to be really good. I have to be awfully good. Then I can go to London." Charles tilts his head and looks at me. "I'll miss you though." Olive has been hunting for men recently, at our soirées. She's looking for a husband, though she'll never admit it. Getting married, having children, gradually slipping into our parents' habits—the boys don't have to do that. They can do exactly as they like. I wet my arms, then wade out of the water.

Small birds are singing in the distance. They seem to be Blackbirds, but I can't quite hear them. Charles is listening too. "You're not allowed to eat any little birds, do you hear?" I say as he hops around me. He gives me a little look. "I do understand why. Margie is so beautiful. I just thought…" Charles flies some distance away, pecks at an insect. I sit down and wipe the dirt from the soles of my feet before putting my shoes on. "…that he understood me."

STAR 3

In the early spring of 1946 an unknown Great Tit and her mate moved into my garden from my neighbour's garden on the west side. She took possession of the nest box on the oak tree, beside the path that leads to my house. She had a small, white, star-shaped patch on her forehead, and moved with exceptional elegance. I called her Star. The regular visitors to my garden kept the new couple at a distance and I would only see them in passing.

In the summer of 1949 she lost her mate and set her heart on Baldhead instead. Baldhead had always lived in my garden. He was a robust, sturdy little Great Tit who completely trusted me. Star did not instantly charm him. He had a mate already, whom I called Monocle, because of the white rim around her left eye, and at first he regarded Star as nothing more than a troublemaker. She was very persistent, however. First she chased Monocle away and then she pursued Baldhead for the whole of that autumn, until halfway through the winter she finally won his heart.

Together they launched a battle against Inkey, Baldhead's old enemy, for possession of Baldhead's former nest box at the side of the house. Inkey was to blame for Baldhead's bald head and his lame foot—when Great Tits fight they sometimes lock their claws together and roll over the ground until one of them has the other on its back and in its grip. The conflict between these two birds had started when they first came as youngsters to the garden, and it flared up again each spring. The feathers that Baldhead lost last year, in his continuous fights with Inkey, did grow back again, but the enmity remained as fierce as ever. Baldhead lost the war last year because Monocle had let him do all the fighting. This year, however, he had Star at his side and the outcome was very different. Star fought against Smoke, Inkey's partner, and although these two were equally matched in physical terms, Star was much more tenacious. Baldhead, however, was not really able to do battle with Inkey because of his lame foot. Instead of this he would swoop down whenever Inkey came too close to their nest, and call as loudly and fiercely as possible to warn him off. In the end, because of their determination and strong characters, Star and Baldhead won back the nest box.

Monocle returned in the early spring, but Star chased her off so forcefully that she almost never came back to the garden again. Instead she retreated some distance away and nested with a younger bird. Her new mate, Peetur, became friends with Baldhead and the two males would often forage in each other's territories. The females, however, maintained their distance. If she caught sight of Star, Monocle would sometimes hide herself under the hair in the nape of my neck. She knew me very well, in fact, and trusted me, because when she was still Baldhead's mate she would often come inside the house. There are some Great Tits who readily trust me, and others whose trust I shall never win. These birds are also more introverted in their relationships with other Great Tits. But birds can learn trust from each other. When Star was living in the nest box by the path she was still quite afraid of humans, but because Baldhead was so fond of me, it was not long before she trusted me too.

1911

"Gwendolen? Will you play the Mozart suite this evening?"

I shake my head.

"Why ever not?" My mother gives me a surprised look, her eyes deliberately widened, the look she turns on men: she knows nothing at all, do enlighten her, give her a hand.

"I always have to play." I walk away from her, into the garden, into the late August warmth.

"Pardon me, young lady, but that's not how it goes. We're counting on you." She follows me, the heels of her white shoes sinking into the damp earth. "Gwen, wait a moment." My mother takes hold of my face with both her hands. "What's wrong with you these days?"

"Nothing." I push her damp hands away from my face.

"But I know you, darling." I smell the sherry on her breath (strange how something from the outer world enters the body, then still wants to get back out) and I take a step backwards. I understand. I'd also go mad with boredom. She holds her hands in the air a moment, as if to indicate the shape of my face. "We're worried about you."

"I want to study music. In London."

"I realise that, sweetheart. Let's talk about it next week, when your father's here." Newman is in London at present, seeing his publisher. "Not that he'll have anything useful to say." She attempts a sideways step, totters. A heel is still stuck in the earth. "Give me a hand then."

"Mrs Howard. Let me help you back into the house." Dimitri gives my mother an arm, me a wink. He coaxes her back over the cockleshell path. Muffled footsteps, then crunching.

In the conservatory Paul's face is bright among the other faces. I pretend I can't see him.

"Gwen, are you playing tonight? Dimitri's going to read his work. Me too. New stuff." He puts a hand on my shoulder.

"No, I haven't studied enough this week."

He takes his hand away. I can still feel its imprint. "This is my sister, Patricia."

The young woman standing by his side looks like him. Her eyes are just as bright as his. She has a bobbed hairstyle, as is the mode now. "Pleased to meet you. I've heard so much about you." She has just arrived and is staying with Paul.

Dimitri joins us. He drains his glass in a single gulp.

"Nervous?" I ask him.

His face flushes. "A little, yes."

"Don't worry. They're tipsy and will think everything is marvellous. Everyone's bored to death here, you know. The tedium of Aberdovey and Towyn has stunned their senses."

He lets out a high-pitched giggle and picks up his folder of poems. His hand is trembling. "I ought to give them another look."

All around us people are conversing, glancing over shoulders, searching for better people to chat with—the conversations are all about neighbours, love affairs, everything that's off limits, and never about why those limits exist.

"Ladies and gentlemen. It's almost half past eight. We're about to begin."

Once everyone is seated, Paul opens the performance. His eyes search the rows—I haven't spotted Margie either. He smiles at me, almost conspiratorially, then smiles at his sister.

Dimitri is second. His voice is gravelly, deeper than you'd expect for his physique. My foot has gone to sleep. I shift my leg, trying to get rid of the sensation. He watches me do so. The paper trembles in his hand. The door opens. Margie slips in as quietly as possible. Dimitri stutters, seems to lose his thread. She walks over to my mother, whispers something in her ear, then beckons me.

"Where is he?" my mother is saying to Olive, in the hallway.

"In hospital. He's unconscious. They don't understand what's wrong with his leg. It doesn't seem broken, but he's got no feeling in it." My sister gasps out the words, high-pitched.

"Dudley's had an accident," Margie says. "He dived off a cliff and landed on a rock, not far from where we were sailing." The wall is near me. I place my hand on its cool stone. "He fell onto the base of his spine. His leg is broken."

My mother's face drains. "We must go now, but someone has to warn Newman."

"You go with Olive," Margie says, "and Gwen and I will look after things here."

"I want to visit Dudley too," I say, feeling dizzy.

"But they won't let three people visit him at once."

Olive leaves with Mother. The sound of applause rings out. I open the door, see Dimitri bow, his poems falling from his hand. Margie goes and stands with him. "Ladies and gentlemen, Florence has asked me to thank you for your presence. There has unfortunately been an accident, so there will be no more refreshments here tonight. Please leave now and go home. Thank you."

"What is the matter?" a man with a deep voice calls out.

"We're not exactly sure."

"Has she fallen ill?"

"Florence is in good health. Thank you. Please save further talk for outside."

I leave the house and stand behind the little wall that encloses the veranda, waiting till everyone has gone. The garden seems to reach further than before—it's a darker green. Things will never be the same again. Restlessness creeps over me, coils around me like ivy. The back door opens. Dimitri steps onto the veranda. He leans his elbows on the wall. It will mark his skin.

"Have they gone now?" The lights are on in the house, as if something else is about to happen.

He jumps. "Blimey, Gwen. Where did you spring from?" He gives a high-pitched laugh, then lights a cigarette.

"Do you know where Kingsley is?"

"He'll be with his girl."

Kingsley usually shows up in the course of the evening, though he's not keen on music or poetry. His place is out of doors, not inside. My mother used to call him "The Changeling", but now she doesn't call him anything at all.

"Did the rest of your performance go well?" I flap my hands to shake out the fear.

"No. But at least I did it." He looks at me. "Your brother will be all right. He's as hard as nails." He gives me his cigarette.

I draw on it and inhale. It irritates my throat and I try not to cough.

Dimitri takes the cigarette back.

A Blackbird lands in a sycamore behind him and begins to sing.

"Shouldn't that Blackbird be asleep? It's far too late for music."

"They're talking to each other."

"Like you with your violin."

Dimitri puts the cigarette on the wall and takes a step towards me. I stay where I am, standing straight, and close my eyes till I feel his breath.

The smell of brilliantine, smoke, his lips, the hairs above them, he's gentle with me, then greedy, it lasts a minute, two, I stop counting, the Blackbird is still singing, I'm dizzy, his hand on my arm, my back, my body is alive, my hand is asleep, it's as if all my feelings are on my skin or inside my skin. I take a step back, see Dimitri open his eyes, see a look in them that I don't know but do understand, then I go inside.

In my room I undress myself, layer by layer, my body feeling strange and tingling. I open the window, dressed in my nightgown. "Charlie," I call. "Charlie." I can't call loudly. Everyone is asleep now. Just as I'm on the point of closing the window I hear the beat of his wings. He perches on the windowsill. "Come on," I say. He settles onto the edge of the bed. I gently stroke his back, even though I know he doesn't like this. Weariness grips me, replacing the tension. Charles takes a sideways step, plucks at his feathers. "Sorry, Charlie. Dudley's in hospital. It was such a strange evening." I tell him about Dimitri. Perhaps he already knows. From the sky he sees everything.

He stays in the room until I fall asleep. I almost wake from the beat of his wings as he leaves, a black scratch across my dream.

*   *   *

As I'm returning from the hospital I see Patricia sitting on the wall in front of our house.

"Hallo." She jumps down. "How's your brother?"

"They're operating on him now. My parents are with him."

"Was it a terrible shock for you?"

"Not too bad."

She gives me a questioning look.

"I have to go in," I tell her.

"All right. I understand. I just wanted to find out how things are for you."

I walk to the front door.

"Are you busy this evening?"

I turn to face her. "Sorry. I've hardly slept and I'm awfully tired."

"Tomorrow then?"

The wind rises, blows my coat open. She's still standing there, as if she has the right to something.

"All right."

"I'll come and fetch you."

She runs off, like a child, in the direction of the park. In the field beside her a Partridge flies up. She moves like her brother does, taking large strides.

"Hallo," I call out in the hallway. No answer. I go to the grand piano in the sitting room and open the lid. I play 'Chopsticks', *Für Elise* and then, three times, the first parts of Mozart's 'Turkish March' in far too slow a tempo. I love playing the piano, but the others don't like it when I do because I make too many mistakes. I slip up more when they watch my fingers. When I stop playing I hear applause. Cook is standing in the doorway watching me. "How beautifully you play, dearie." Her accent seamlessly threads the words together. I go to her and fling my arms around her. She smells so safe, so familiar—of bread and meat and sweat—and she cuddles me as if I'm still a little girl.

* * *

In the morning the oak leaves are blowing against my window. It's not yet autumn, not even late summer, but the fleecy clouds above the garden scurry by and the day already holds the coming months within it: long rainy Sundays, cold walks on the beach and boxes with injured Pigeons inside them, too weak to survive the winter, though sometimes they do.

Mother isn't at breakfast. I go and sit next to Olive.

"And couldn't you let us know? Your brother is in hospital." My father's voice fills the hallway. Kingsley mutters something. "Yes, I know he isn't dead. But as long as you live under my roof you remain a part of this family."

Kingsley comes into the dining room with lowered head, bags under his eyes, uncombed hair. Papa's face is red with pent-up fury and his right hand tightly clasps a pen. They both have exactly the same angry expression on their faces.

My father pulls back a chair, almost missing it as he sits down. When I look at Olive we both start laughing, so I concentrate on my toast and suppress a giggle. The lump of jam on the bread looks like a flop-eared puppy. I spread the puppy out, eat it in silence, hiccup only once.

"Are you going to practise now?" my father asks as I stand.

I nod. I should really be studying two new pieces for tomorrow—the Haydn is going well, but the Mozart is pretty difficult, or at any rate fast, and I've spent too little time on it.

I meet my mother on the staircase. She takes me in her arms and presses my head against her shoulder. She holds me just a little too tight.

"Mama," I say, and wriggle free.

I go up the stairs two steps at a time: the music is already in my head.

On my bed I tune up and think about Dimitri, the nervy one. I don't want to marry him or be his girl. Do I want to see him again? I play a little melody to warm up my fingers. Perhaps. He wants me.

The Haydn piece starts calmly—my fingers know the way, as far as the modulation. I search for the correct positions, think without thinking, do it all by touch, play what isn't right till it's nearly right. Notes give shape to other people's thoughts, from former times, become mine, allow my thoughts to disappear, change them into music.

After an hour I put the violin down, its strings resting on the blankets, and search for the Mozart piece in my sheet music—my left hand is already working the fingering out on the bed. I look at the oak tree by the window, the ancient bark, and feel its form inside my fingers; the branches are pointing at the window and every now and then they let a leaf fall—green leaves with brown edges. Trees carry the whole year within them, broken into pieces by the seasons. A day is broken into pieces by appointments, words, promises, thoughts. A street is broken into pieces by footsteps, houses, poplars (houses for Blackbirds, for Blue Tits).

My eyes are drawn to the garden wall, where there's a little figure sitting, biting her nails.

I'd forgotten all about her.

I open the window. "Hey! Have you been sitting there long?" My voice wafts back into the room.

Patricia stands, waves at me. "Are you coming?"

The window closes itself. I only have to step back from it.

"Are you here on holiday?" I ask.

"More or less. My parents are fed up of me and Paul has an extra room. They want me to get married after the summer and they've even decided who it'll be."

She doesn't really look like Paul but she has the same expression—eyes screwed up a little, a small frown. "Who, then?"

"Shall we go to the beach?"

"It's rather windy."

"Exactly! Want a ciggie?"

"I don't smoke."

"You're only young once." She takes a cigarette from a tin case.

"What's it like in London?" We're walking down the gravel path towards the pebble beach. There's a green haze on the white wall behind us, solidified sea breath.

"Just as boring as here. That is to say: there's enough to do, but not enough breathing space. Everyone knows everyone else. If ever you do anything you mustn't do, then everyone knows about it immediately. Certainly if you're a woman." She pulls her left shoe off. "Ow."

"I'd keep your shoes on a while, if I were you. A little further on it turns to sand."

She gives me the shoe, which is warm—the leather soft, someone's skin—and leans her hand on my shoulder as she brushes fragments of shell from her foot with her other hand.

"So they want me to get married." She hesitates. "To someone I had a relationship with. But all he wants is a beautiful wife to match his beautiful house."

"I'll never marry." As I say it I know that it's true.

She laughs. "What will you do then?"

"I'll study music. I want to play in an orchestra. What about you?"

"I'm going to be a writer." She looks exultant, but also a little earnest.

"I used to write stories about the birds in the garden. But who'd want to read about birds?"

"I'd like to read those stories." She takes my arm. I get goose bumps.

We're walking across the narrow ledge, past the boats and towards the sandy beach. Light-blue water shifts into dark blue, into dark-blue sky. I tell her I'm afraid of words sometimes, because they trap things that you'd better not trap—it's much easier to say what I mean with the violin. She says it can't be words that frighten me, because words are just husks, carriers of something else.

Meanwhile the sun breaks the clouds in two above the horizon, a mouth speaking light, smiling at the margins.

*   *   *

One day Dudley is there when I come home from my violin lesson. He is sitting in a chair by the window, gazing at the garden. "Hallo, Duddie. It's good to see you home again." My voice sounds strangely polite.

"I'm pleased to be home too." He keeps staring out of the window, as if something is happening outside. But only the grass is moving, and the shrubs.

"How's your leg now?"

"No idea."

Cook rings the bell. Tea is ready. I go upstairs to put away my violin. Mike is singing in the garden. Ta-da-da, tada.

Dudley sits opposite me at teatime. His eyes continue to avoid mine and he doesn't speak to anyone. Mother talks: about the neighbour, whom she suspects of having a love affair, about an argument with her sister, about an evening playing cards with her friend, who was being frightfully peevish. Father comes to sit with us a while, mutters something about a poem he started composing last night, and then leaves again.

When Cook brings the sandwiches, Mother clasps her forehead. "It's doing it again. I must go to bed." Cook fetches Tessa from the kitchen to help my mother up the stairs.

Dudley takes a sandwich from the plate. He chews with his lips slightly open, so that his mouth acts like a sound box. He eats sluggishly, bite by bite: before humans were able to speak they chewed at each other. Cook pours the tea for us. I can feel Olive looking at me, but I don't look sideways—the laughter is already bubbling up. Dudley doesn't seem to notice. He takes a fairy cake. Crumbs linger in his moustache, falling beside his plate at every bite.

"You're making a mess," Olive says, pressing her lips together.

He takes another little cake, and this time he deliberately brushes the crumbs out of his moustache, dropping them by his plate.

"Ugh," I say.

"Ugh," he says. "Do you know what's disgusting? Your sham sympathy. It doesn't matter two hoots to you whatever happens. You just think about your violin." He turns to Olive. "And you just want to fit in. Mimicking Mother. That's what you enjoy."

I take a bite from my sandwich and think about the Mozart. I can play it in my head now and usually my hands are swift to follow. Dudley licks a finger, brushes it across the table so that the crumbs stick to it, licks it clean. And again.

Olive pushes her chair back. The legs give a little hop on the wooden floor. There is a half-eaten sandwich on her plate, a waxing moon.

Before I stand I look briefly at Dudley. His eyes are calm, as if he has said nothing at all. He helps himself to another cake.

*   *   *

"I've come to say goodbye." Patricia steps out of the shadow of the oak tree. "You don't have to come with me."

"But I jolly well can," I say.

She picks up the big suitcase. I take the small one. We walk through the light towards the darkness. Beyond the curve the path by the railway line is roofed with branches. She tells me about her plans for when she is back in London, about her book. I tell her about the new piece I'm studying, a Chopin waltz. Little stones are shifted by our feet, stones that perhaps are seldom shifted. A train passes, and then it's quiet again—only ducks quacking in the distance and the wind making the grass rustle.

"You'll have to take matters into your own hands. Otherwise time will simply slip by. Otherwise you'll become what they expect you to be. Then you'll turn into your mother."

I shake my head.

"Chin up." She taps below my chin. "You should give Stockdale a ring."

The train approaches, brakes, stops at the top end of the platform. We run towards it. She buys a ticket from the guard and I embrace her. "It's a shame you have to leave so soon."

"I'll be back. Or we'll see each other in London."

"You know, I—"

"Yes?"

The guard blows his whistle, signals to her to hurry. She steps in.

"What did you want to say?"

"Nothing. It'll be all right."

She walks through the carriage, sits by the window, places her hand on the pane. I lay my hand against it till I feel the train moving.

I wave and wave until the train has completely disappeared. The sun has changed position. I walk back in the light. I'm not wearing a hat and my parting is burning.

I telephone Stockdale from the post office.

"Who's speaking?"

"It's Gwen. Gwen Howard."

"Oh, I'm so sorry, Gwen. I didn't hear you properly. Very nice of you to ring me. Is everything all right?"

"Yes, thank you. Everything's fine. I just wanted to ask you something. I'd like to study at the College of Music, but my parents aren't all that keen. My father has a very high opinion of you and I think he'd listen to you. So, I was hoping that…"

"I'd put in a word for you. Of course. But on one condition."

"And that is?"

"That you'll play in my orchestra."

My smile glides over the post office counter, lights up the floor and the walls.

"Oh, yes please."

"Good. Well, I'll set things in motion then."

I thank him and leave the post office with red cheeks. I don't walk home, veer off before I reach our street and follow the shell path beside the railway, past the white hotels, to the harbour, and then carry on towards the sea. I steal an apple from an apple tree, keep walking as far as the sandy beach, then sit down in a cleft in the cliff side. The water, the far horizon, the taste of the apple—I really want to sing, but instead I sit here and let the sound of the water wash over me, wave after wave.

STAR 4

In March Star began to prepare her nesting box. She flew back and forth for days with bark, moss, strands of fibre and other soft materials. She did this as she did everything: with dedication and passion. These characteristics were apparent not only in her behaviour, her thoroughness: her whole posture was full of concentration, like a musician playing.

Baldhead regarded the nest as his territory and when Star had finally finished her nest-making, he would turn up every night to sleep there. Star chased him off. Raising a brood is demanding enough as it is, and an extra sleeper means extra cleaning. But Baldhead was persistent and flitted around the nest box each evening, singing and calling until she gave in. Star would sit inside the box, blocking the entrance, holding her head to one side, as if assessing his song. He must have made at least thirty attempts on the first night, but this decreased each day, as if they both knew that Star would eventually give in. So Baldhead slept in the nest box until the nestlings were a few days old. Then of his own accord he looked for another roost.

Five days after the babies had hatched, Star came to me to fetch food for them. Before that she had given her youngsters only natural food; what she took from me was simply for herself. She was hastier than normal that day and flew back to the nest box a number of times while I was busy in the kitchen. Baldhead arrived an hour after her. He flew straight to me and nestled down on my lap; his little legs were too weak to let him stand. As soon as she saw him Star left the nest box and came to us. She tried to encourage him to go with her, ardently quivering her wings and calling to him. He cheeped a little but otherwise lay still. She returned a few more times that afternoon, the last time simply gazing at him a moment from a distance.

From that time onwards she played the biggest role in feeding their brood. Baldhead would sometimes take a piece of bread from the bird table to the nest, but would then sleep again for a few more hours. His favourite roost was on my lap, where he would come for a peanut, supposedly. He would then press his little head against my tummy and stay there. Sometimes he would not even eat his nut.

1914

"Come with me then."

Olive is sitting on my bed, watching me pack. "If Papa also has to enlist at some point, then I'll have to help Mama with the house and with Dudley."

"Mama can take care of Dudley by herself, surely?"

Olive raises an eyebrow. Since the accident Mother has started drinking in the afternoons again. Father, however, has stopped. He shuts himself in his room all day to work on his poems about the war. Last year his *Collected Poems* were published, a milestone that has mainly made him feel discontented. "It's all rubbish. It's all got to change." Since then all he ever does is write. He doesn't even watch the birds now.

"You don't have to sacrifice yourself, you know."

Olive stares out of the window. "Anyway, I don't know what else I could do. I'm good for nothing."

I sit beside my sister.

"There isn't a single man who'd want me, because I'm too ugly. Pure and simple. And too old. And I can't do anything at all."

"You can play the piano. And sew. And you're really quick." Olive can run like the wind. She leaves Kingsley far behind.

"What's the point of that? I'm twenty-six." She laughs, but her eyes are still sad.

"Do you want me to stay?"

"No, of course not." She takes my hand, squeezes it a little, then puts it back where it was before—a used tool.

Charles is perched on the windowsill. He taps the pane with his beak. I open the window for him.

"Are you letting that filthy Crow in?"

Charles perches on the bed, then flies to the desk when Olive moves towards him. He's quite happy there. He knows that Olive never stays very long.

"I'm getting older too," I say.

"You're still young. And it's different in London." She stands up. "I'll go and see if Mama is all right. I've heard nothing from her all day."

Charles comes and joins me. He acquired a mate last year, a very clever Crow. She's a little smaller than the others but twice as sharp. I stroke his head and then carry on with my packing. I've already put my clothes in the suitcase, the other half of it is for my sheet music. I have to take the famous pieces, at any rate, and a few personal favourites as well. I put them in, take them out, put them back again. Charles hops onto the bookcase. I'd really like to pack all the bird books I've collected over the years, but that would be at the cost of my music. I can fetch them at Christmas. And in London I can always use a library.

My notebooks are on the top shelf. I leaf through them—stories about Charles, about Bennie the Magpie, who lived in my father's study for a whole year; botched attempts at notating birdsong; lists of the birds who visited our garden last summer. At the summer's end our neighbour came to tea and asked what always kept me busy in the garden. "She writes down which birds come to visit," my mother said, and then they both started giggling. I set the notebooks down beside my suitcase. It would be better to throw them away.

Kingsley knocks on the open door. "Are you nearly ready? We have to leave at a quarter past six tomorrow morning. Papa and Olive are coming to the station too, to help with the cases." He's letting his beard grow, and looks even more like Father now.

"Exciting, isn't it?" I was going to leave home last year, but suddenly my parents decided I was too young for it. I'm twenty-one now and they can't stop me any more.

He laughs at my enthusiasm; the air of dissatisfaction he always carries with him vanishes a while. "I'm going to miss the chaps, though." He has a large group of friends, young men from the village he meets for sports and drinking.

"Perhaps it's different for a boy."

He gives me a wink. "I've promised them I'll keep an eye on you."

A half-smile, and then I turn back to my suitcase. He probably won't be in London for long. Most of the soldiers are sent to the Continent, to Belgium and France.

The sun suddenly breaks through. The birch tree opposite my window throws its shadow across the bed, across my suitcase. Cook rings the bell for teatime, swift shrill stabs. I run downstairs.

The table is lavishly spread: pots of jam and butter and cream; plates filled with cake, scones, muffins, sandwiches and pancakes. And there's tea and cocoa.

"What a feast!" I sit beside my father.

"Two of my little ones are flying the nest. That calls for a celebration."

I help myself to a muffin. "Olive, pass the strawberry jam, please. And the clotted cream."

She pushes them towards me, stony-faced.

"Is something wrong?"

"Why should anything be wrong? Don't be silly."

"You can always come and visit."

Dudley wolfs down the pancakes as if his life depended on it. He spreads them thickly with butter and jam, or puts cheese and ham on them, rolling them up and cutting them into big chunks. They vanish into his mouth bite by bite. At pancake number five I see Mother stare at him. At number six she says his name. At number seven she gestures to Cook to take the pancakes away. "Hang on," Kingsley says, "I'd like another one."

"Just one, then," Mother says. She takes one from the dish, and puts it on Kingsley's plate, stretching her arm across the table.

"I'm awfully hungry, Mama. I'd like two," he says.

She picks up another one. Her lips form a straight line. Cook asks if anyone else would like a pancake.

"*I'd* like another," Dudley says.

"Should you really?" Mother asks him.

Father taps her hand with his fingers, then taps his fork on the table top. "Don't grudge the lad his pleasures."

"He's eaten six already."

Seven.

My father turns his attention back to his own plate.

"Delicious," he tells Cook. "You've excelled yourself again. What a sumptuous feast! Splendid."

Dudley belches. He swiftly places a napkin in front of his mouth. "Sorry."

"Ugh," Olive says.

Cook coughs. She's still standing there, dish in hand.

"All right then," says Mother.

Dudley treats this pancake exactly like the previous one, but the butter is spread thicker and the jam too.

I can feel Olive looking at me as I take a bite from my scone. I don't return her glance.

The following morning I knock at my mother's door before we leave. She doesn't open it. "Perhaps she isn't well," Olive says.

I push the door handle down. "It's locked."

"Len," my father calls up from the bottom of the stairs. "We really must leave."

I knock one more time.

"Come on," Olive says. I follow her downstairs. My suitcase is heavy, but I want to carry it myself.

*   *   *

The first thing I see when I wake up is my violin, in an open case across two chairs at the foot of the bed. The room is narrow and dark and perfect. Somewhere in the distance a clock is striking. I count along, to seven. I get out of bed and open the window, then sit on the sill with my violin, softly plucking the strings. Trams, voices, wind, the sound of an engine. On the opposite side of the street someone has hung a washing line in front of their window. Underclothes are pegged to it. The rehearsal won't take place till two. I have plenty of time to explore. Someone knocks at the door and I hurriedly put on my dressing gown.

"Miss Howard? Good morning. My name is Sylvia. Mrs Sewell asked me to wake you. Breakfast will be ready at half past seven." Sylvia is shorter than me by a head. She's wearing a white cap perched on flaxen hair. She can't be more than sixteen.

I get dressed and braid my own hair. The door from the room beside mine opens and then closes—it isn't half past seven yet, but I'm hungry.

Mrs Sewell is standing at the bottom of the dark wooden staircase. She's talking to a tall young lady with curly red hair. "No, by Friday," she says sharply. "This is your last chance."

The young lady turns abruptly, gives me a brief look, winks and walks away. She's wearing lipstick.

"Good morning, Miss Howard. Did you sleep well?" Mrs Sewell is all smiles with me. "The dining room is over there."

I walk across the thick dark-brown carpet to the back room, where the girl I've just seen is sitting alone at the table.

"Would you mind if I sat beside you?"

She laughs. "Please do. I'm Thea." She takes my right hand with her left hand, clasping her teacup firmly in her right.

"Gwendolen, but they call me Gwen. Or Len."

"Hallo Len, welcome to the Haunted House. That's what we all call it. The only real spectre here is Mrs Sewell, but still." She gives a Cheshire Cat grin. "Are you a musician too?"

"I play the violin. What about you?"

"Jolly good, then we can play together. Cello." Freckles form a pathway, fanning out from her nose to her cheeks. I look dark and pale beside her, lacking in colour.

"Do you also play in an orchestra?"

"I have three auditions this week. Hopefully something will come of them, otherwise things will get a little awkward. Money-wise too." She pours more milk into her cup and drinks the tepid tea in a single gulp. "Something always turns up. Till now, at least."

"I've been engaged by the Queen's Hall Orchestra."

"Phew, you're good then. So much the better! I say, do you have a young man?"

I shake my head, help myself to some toast and spread it with butter and jam. "What about you?"

"Two, at the moment. Andrew, who's a soldier, and Johnny, from the last orchestra I played in. That's the reason they threw me out. They don't want us to mix love and work. Just so you know."

"My brother is a soldier."

"Is he good-looking?" Her eyes open wider, as if she's searching for him in me.

"No idea. Now, I'd like to explore the neighbourhood after breakfast. Do you want to come along?"

She grimaces. "Why are you bothered about this place? Come into town with me. Do you know London already?"

"Not really."

"Marvellous. Then I'll guide you, and you're in luck, 'cos I'm the best guide ever!"

*   *   *

"Bring your coat. It's going to rain." Thea is waiting for me at the bottom of the stairs. I run back up, almost bumping into the landlady.

"Miss Howard?"

"Excuse me. I was in a hurry."

"We do not run on the staircase in this establishment."

I offer my apologies once again.

Thea laughs at my crestfallen face. "Mrs Sewell isn't so bad. She can sometimes hit the roof, but she's helped me out of a fix a couple of times. This time too. I haven't paid her for two weeks in a row. Anyone else would've thrown me out long ago."

"Do you want to borrow some cash?"

"Rule one: never ask a stranger if she needs to borrow cash. No one here has any money, especially the musicians. Save your cash for a rainy day." She combs her hand through her curls. "We're going that way, through the park. You been to London before?"

"A long time ago." The ground beneath our feet is moving. A heavy wagon rolls along, right beside us. I can smell the horse's body. Thea doesn't seem to notice it. "Have you lived here long?"

"I was born here. My parents moved to Scotland when I was thirteen. I moved in with an aunt and uncle. I didn't want to go with my parents."

A motor vehicle, with an open-top deck, comes towards us—the soldiers inside it call out to Thea. She sees me staring.

"They're the new buses. They use them as transport for our boys now. Perhaps your brother's inside it. They certainly fancy you."

"They're calling to you!"

"To both of us. You're still a bit green, aren't you?" I look aside, and she laughs.

The bus leaves tracks in the mud, traces in the air. There's a policeman at the crossroads, sternly gesturing at us to wait.

"Take it easy," Thea tells him. "It's her first day in London."

The man smiles, suddenly ten years younger. "Welcome to London, miss." He lets us cross.

Thea tells me that she can't choose between Andrew and Johnny, because they're both so handsome. Andrew is manly and Johnny plays beautifully. She thinks she perhaps likes Johnny best. I gaze around. The houses are so tall and the street is filthy, black with dirt, fumes, horse droppings. "Don't they ever clean the streets here?"

"The sweepers come every morning!"

Our route becomes a path through a park. There's a man sitting on a bench with his eyes closed, tattered trousers, no coat or shoes. Thea pulls me along. "Tramp," she says, when we're out of earshot. By the park exit there are two more of them. Thea acts as if she hasn't seen them. They do exactly the same. Then we turn right—low houses with washing lines strung between them, pegged with cotton clothing: white shirts, dresses, long johns. When we get closer I can see how many times they've been mended. White on lighter white.

In the shopping street she tells me about the last orchestra she played in, and asks again if we can play together. She says work is scarce, that I've been lucky. "I hope it goes well for you. That Stockdale has a bit of a temper." We look at the shop windows, untouched by the war: thousands of kinds of soap, silk dresses, jewellery. "Will you have a drink with me?"

She indicates a door with wooden ornamentation, gold-leaf paint and green glass.

"Sorry. I have to rehearse pretty soon."

She asks if I can find my way home and embraces me, as if we're already very good friends. Then she enters the pub and I'm left alone in a city that bids me a reluctant welcome. Two Crows are chattering to each other, high in a poplar tree. I feel a pain grip my stomach. Charles will have no idea where I've gone, or why.

*   *   *

The rehearsal room is in a former school building. It has high windows and an even higher ceiling. Today only the strings are rehearsing. I shake hands, forget names, a smile on my face. The butterflies aren't just in my stomach, but in my fingertips too. A bony woman with mousy hair, who had introduced herself as Joan, starts to tune up and soon everyone is softly playing, all higgledy-piggledy, a patchwork of tonalities and random themes. My music stand is stiff, won't open. I tug and wrench at it, my face growing red. I can see a tall man in a brightly coloured shirt look enquiringly at me—and then, thank goodness, it springs open. The sheet music stays in place, the violin is only a little out of tune, and then I also start warming up, long low lines that climb softly higher—I let the sound disappear into everyone else's.

"Are we all ready?" Stockdale casts his eye over the whole troupe. There's a young woman beside me with light-blonde curly hair and sea-grey eyes. She's wearing a frock that seems far too good for a rehearsal. She sits down on one of the wooden chairs. I take the seat beside her. "I'm Billie," she whispers. "Welcome!"

"I think you've all met Gwendolen by now. She's joining the violins."

I give him a nod and nod to those around me. I gaze at the ground again and try to swallow, but my mouth is too dry. Behind me someone gives a loud, prolonged cough.

"Right. Haydn. Father of the symphony. Roman Catholic. Nasal polyps. Pocky face. Didn't even die young."

He carries on talking about the piece we'll play. I bite my lip and practise my fingering. My entry comes later. I don't have to do anything special, just play with everyone else and count well. The first violin begins to play, four bars, eight, and then we come in, at the right point, and I have the feeling that I'm being lifted up, that we're lifting something together, higher and higher.

"Yes. Stop. Priscilla, you're playing much too fast. Gwen, I can't hear you. Somewhat louder, please. Joan, a little quicker." I wipe the palm of my hand against my skirt.

And again, and again. My heart begins to beat more calmly. I can hear the others better now. I start to sense when I have to come in, though I keep counting in my head, to be on the safe side.

When it's over my fingers are tingling and my cheeks and ears are red. Voices ring through the room, cases are snapped shut. I smile at the woman with the curly hair and, carrying my violin, leave the room in my new shoes that are hurting my feet a little. From now on it will only get better.

*   *   *

"Are you coming for a drink with us?" Billie asks, picking up her violin case. I follow her to the hotel bar, past wicker baskets piled high in front of the laundry. On the other side of the street a girl is walking. She looks like Olive. She's just as tall and blonde. If only Olive could see what it's like here. Yesterday I sent her a long letter. I hope she'll write back soon.

It's dark in the bar-room. My colleagues are already sitting in the corner. Coloured light falls through the stained-glass windows onto the round wooden table. I sit beside Priscilla. The velvet of the upholstered bench is so plush it barely dents. Stockdale asks us what we'd like to drink. I'm the only one who asks for tea. "Don't you drink?" Billie, who is on my other side, asks me.

"I want to get up early tomorrow morning to practise." And I still have to get home, without getting lost or being bothered by unwanted attentions.

"Sensible. I was like that too, you know, at the start. You'll soon adapt."

The barmaid puts a tray on the table. Stockdale picks up his whisky. "Cheers. Health to the men, and may the women live for ever!"

"At least it's still well stocked here," Priscilla says, taking a large sip of sherry. "Most of the other places don't have hardly any proper stuff now. Because of the bloody war." Her cockney accent modifies the words, making them somehow plumper and sturdier: chubby, cheeky toddlers.

Billie leans across to her. "Have you any idea what happened to Marion? Did that young man really put her in the family way?"

I must be giving her a questioning look, since she starts to tell me that Marion was my predecessor, a good violin player, but a little too easy.

Stockdale grabs a chair and pushes it between Priscilla and me. "How have you found your first week?" I can smell his sweat, his breath.

"It's been good. But I'm exhausted." I shuffle a little towards the wall, but there's not much space left.

"Don't be scared. Fatherly concern, you know. I've promised Newman to keep an eye on you, and that's what I'll do. Like a dog with a bone." They were at boarding school together and both of them were outsiders. They've been friends ever since. Father finds much to criticise in him, but says he's a sterling fellow nevertheless.

The tea is still too hot to drink. I should have asked for water. And I don't know who will pay for it. "I didn't bring my purse. I'm sorry. I forgot."

"I always pay for the first round. But only on Fridays, and only if we're not performing in the evening. I'm pleased you've come, Gwen. You're an asset to the orchestra. If there's any problem at all, you know you can always call on me."

He gives me a little pat, as if I'm a good pet, and then moves on to Sonia, a Russian clarinettist who is in London for six months, at the orchestra's invitation. She wears red lipstick and a tight black dress. Stockdale sees me watching and gives a wink before he turns to her.

* * *

On my first free day I go to Hyde Park. It's a long way from my lodgings, an hour and a half's walk, but I miss the birds. There are only two sycamore trees in my street, and although the small parks in my neighbourhood do attract some birds— Pigeons, Crows, the odd Blackbird or Sparrow, and of course Starlings—most of them live elsewhere. I bought birdseed with my first pay, and put some of it on the windowsill, only to have to brush it off a few days later. But I kept the rest in my handbag and when I see Pigeons in the neighbourhood I strew some on the ground for them. The days are growing shorter. There's frost at nights and they're hungry.

Hyde Park isn't a wood, but there are plenty of oaks and beeches and Blackbirds and Sparrows. There's a lake with water lilies, Ducks, Coots, Geese and Swans, and on one of the lawns a group of Greylag Geese are grazing. I walk the restlessness out of my body, then sit down on a bench and take a sandwich from my bag. As I am taking it out of its brown paper, a man comes and sits beside me. The smell of his coat makes me feel queasy. "Would you like a sandwich?" I ask him. He silently accepts it, takes a few bites, leaves the rest on the bench, still in its paper, and walks on. Three Pigeons, two of them grey and one white, land in front of me. I take the bread from the paper and crumble it up. The white one is smaller than the other two and so I give her the most. "All gone," I say, letting them see my empty hands before wiping them on my dress. The Pigeons scratch around a little longer, then fly off, only to land at the next bench where someone is eating.

*   *   *

Mother writes to me each week. In December she announces that she'll come to visit me at Christmas. The day I go to the station to fetch her it's raining cats and dogs. I haven't brought an umbrella with me, only a scarf wrapped around my head. People are sheltering in doorways or waiting in shops where the lights shine brightly. It's the weekend before Christmas and everyone is shopping: handbags, hats, toy trains. The war seems far away, till a motor vehicle laden with soldiers suddenly passes, or until there's no more chocolate some-where, or alcohol.

On the timetable in the station hall I see that my moth-er's train is expected in ten minutes. I wipe the damp, gleaming wood of the bench with my hand before sitting down. Cold creeps into my body and I sneeze, twice. My coat is heavy with rain; the air smells of coats. The sound of trains vibrates through the ground, not their cadence but the braking. I think about the piece that will premiere tomorrow—I left the rehearsal early to meet my mother and I'm not sure I should have allowed myself to do so. It's a piece with many changes of tempo and it needs a delicate touch. But Stockdale certainly thought I should meet her. And he added that he felt a great affection for my mother.

Brighton, Manchester, Edinburgh—it would be so easy to travel elsewhere from here. Movement always bears a promise with it. On stations, in music.

A man in a long black overcoat comes and sits beside me. "Terrible weather, isn't it?" he says. I nod. "All on your lonesome?"

"I'm waiting for my mother."

"Oh indeed. Your mother." He leans towards me. I shuffle along a little. He hawks into a handkerchief.

"Gwennie!" Mother is walking towards me across the smooth station floor. She kisses me on both cheeks. Behind her there's a young man carrying a large suitcase. "This is Jim. He has kindly offered to carry my case for me. Where should I tell him to bring it?"

She talks all the way back to Mrs Sewell's house—about Papa and Olive and Dudley, and about Kingsley too, who has finally sent her a letter, in his usual scrawl. About where she lived in London when she was a little girl. And about the neighbours and the other people in the little town in Wales and how they really are going to move now but not to London, probably back to Surrey again. Stories that are repetitions of other stories. Variations. When you've known someone a long time, then most stories are variations, sometimes with a modulation. I only have to nod, put in an occasional "Hmm", and make sure we're on the right route. Jim walks through the wet city with us, a silent, docile individual, always obediently following two steps behind Mother.

"How may I reward you?" she asks him when we're almost there.

"With a kiss."

Mother hesitates, or pretends to hesitate.

"Just a joke. But please do visit me, tomorrow or the day after." He writes his address on a piece of paper that is immediately soaked by the rain. "Is it still legible?" He presses it into her hand.

Mother nods, then kisses his cheek. Once she's in the house she throws the slip of paper into the wastepaper basket, beside the staircase. She smiles at me. "Come on then. Show me your room."

*　　　*　　　*

We have Christmas lunch at the Criterion. The enormous Christmas tree is decorated with candles and gold ribbons; there are pine branches tied with red ribbon at all the windows. A waiter wearing a shining, golden bow tie takes our coats from us, while a second waiter shows us to our table.

"You were marvellous yesterday, darling," Mother says as soon as we're seated. She said that yesterday too, after the performance, and again as we walked home. "I'm so glad we finally have the time to talk. But I do understand that you have to practise. A performance like that is quite something."

"Would you like to order your drinks, ma'am?"

My mother smiles at the waiter, turning her décolleté towards him. "A glass of champagne. And you, darling?"

"Darjeeling tea, please." The gold mosaic on the ceiling is glittering.

"First Flush then. She's performing this evening. She plays the violin. In the Queen's Hall Orchestra."

The waiter gives my mother a nod, and the sound of his footsteps vanishes into the carpet.

"Things are awfully difficult with Papa, you know. His new book isn't going at all well. He's becoming more and more critical of his work. He labours for weeks at a poem, but then he simply tears it up."

"Perhaps you ought to find something to occupy you too, Mama. Piano. Or painting. Margaret's things are still in the attic." Mother has often told us that she used to be quite a good artist, but we've never seen any evidence of that.

"I have enough to occupy me, as you well know. Organising the soirées, managing everyone. And Cook may leave us in February, to care for her sister—and it won't be easy to replace her. That new maid can't be properly trusted either, so Dolores says, you know, from Towyn. So I have to keep a careful eye on her. And then there's Dudley, who does nothing at all, but constantly criticises everything. And your sister, who can't find a man."

"She'll find one without you. She's very attractive." I pass my hand across my forehead, smoothing away my frown.

"Well, she could try a little harder." She takes a large draught from the glass that the waiter places in front of her. "Anyway, it's good she's still at home. At least she hasn't deserted her poor old mother."

I blow on my tea.

"And how is love treating you?"

"Mama, please." On the table in front of me there's a red napkin with golden stars, folded into a fan.

"But if I don't ask, you don't like it either." She purses her lips. "And you're really quite presentable now."

"I'm too busy for all that."

"Quite presentable still. But you mustn't wait too long."

"The menu, ma'am." The waiter places two menus in front of us. My mother asks him if the lobster is truly as delicious as reputed.

There's a cough from the man at the next table. "If I may be so bold: the lobster is without equal." His voice sounds too high-pitched for his body. He gasps for breath after speaking a few words. His belly touches the edge of the table.

"So, I know what to order then." My mother gives me a triumphant look.

"I'd like to study the menu a little longer." I smile at the waiter, who nods and leaves us.

Our neighbour coughs again. He is wearing a gleaming dress suit and a red bow tie with green dots. "My wife has left me," he says quietly to my mother. "Yesterday. She said she could no longer put up with it."

My mother looks shocked. "With what?"

"Goodness knows." He wipes his mouth with his napkin, then stands up. "Happy Christmas then."

"It is difficult sometimes," my mother says, when he has gone. "He seemed a nice man, but so does your father. Here." She pushes a package towards me. "I was supposed to give you this."

I carefully unwrap the shiny red paper. *Birds of the City and Suburbs*. Line drawings and advice on how to make our environs more welcoming for birds.

"Do the ladies know what they would like to order?" The waiter leans over my mother, who gives him her best smile. I order game pie with Cumberland sauce. I'm not terribly hungry.

At the end of the afternoon I take my mother to her train. As I walk back home it begins to snow at last. With the snow comes solace and expectation. Children are allowed out of doors a while; adults remember that they were once children. The sounds of the city swiftly diminish, become duller, thicker. Dirt disappears into the whiteness. I breathe the cold in, clouds out.

The next morning I get up earlier than usual to make my own tracks, so I can walk without having to follow the tracks of others. A Crow flies cawing overhead—for a moment I miss Charles so intensely that I can hardly breathe. For a moment I miss Olive and my father, even Dudley and everyone else.

When I'm inside the house again, I pick up my violin and use my fingers to search for what I'm feeling. I play until it's over. As long as I do my best, I'll be all right.

*   *   *

After the last performance of the year, we hurry through the rain to the bar. Stockdale orders punch all round. "Well played, all of you."

I hang my coat on the rack and sit down by Billie. She asks if I'll go with them to a New Year's Eve party. Then a gust of wind draws my attention to the door, where a woman in a green coat is entering, arm in arm with a man. Her silhouette seems familiar. I jump up and worm my way through the crowd towards her. She takes off her coat when she reaches the bar. Pearl necklace, gold chain and locket, dark-red frock. "Patricia?"

"Hallo Len." She laughs. "You did it!"

"How wonderful to see you." I embrace her, smelling perfume and cigarettes.

"This is William."

I hold out my hand, and he kisses it, quite the gallant. "My husband." Her tone is a little exaggerated, just short of being affected.

I raise an eyebrow. "Surely not."

"Oh yes. I've caved in. To the charms of this heartbreaker." She turns towards him. "Lennie and I swore that we'd never get married. That was in my wilder days, when all I wanted to do was write." She lays her hand on my arm, and takes my wrist. "I do write," she tells me, my disappointment lying between us like a cloud, visible but not tangible. "I'm writing a manifesto at present, on the position of women in marriage."

"For a year now," William laughs. "For a whole year and nothing to show for it. But when the baby comes, she won't be such a fidget."

She also laughs. "No baby. Definitely not." She taps her finger against his nose. For a moment I see Paul in her—he left for London two years ago, and since then I've heard nothing more of him.

"How is your brother?"

"He's well. He's in Brighton now, by the sea again. His first collection came out last year." She is still holding tightly on to my wrist. I hope she won't let go, and I nod.

"Yes, I've read about the book. It's had good reviews."

"Sorry, I completely forgot to ask how you are. Do you still play the violin, Lennie?"

William spots an acquaintance and excuses himself. She pulls me closer.

"What on earth happened?" I ask her.

"Purist!" She laughs.

"Are you really expecting a child?"

"In his dreams." Perhaps it's not my disappointment, but hers. Perhaps it can be felt, but not seen—wind, not cloud.

"But is everything going well?"

Her grip tightens before she lets go. "Not as well as for you. I've been ill. I'm…" She hesitates. William is coming back. "Not as strong as I'd like to be."

"Are you coming, darling? We should leave now." He places his hand on her back. "We've bought tickets for the cinema," he tells me.

Sound. Sound is something you can feel but not see, unless it moves something else. I lean towards her, kiss her cheek, hold my face beside hers a little too long. She whispers something, but walks away before I can ask her what she means—the music is too loud and everyone is talking at the top of their voices.

He holds her coat open for her, she wriggles herself into it, left arm, right arm, her face turns round further, till she sees mine, and she waves. Waving is unnecessary, so I smile at her and she smiles back.

STAR 5

The Great Tits would generally grasp my meaning very swiftly. If I was at table, eating a sandwich, a couple of them would always come for a look. If I did not react, then they would perch on the plate to take a morsel. If I sternly said no, they flew up. If I moved my hand when I spoke, they would fly away from the table entirely. If I was really cross, they would even fly out of the window. Then if I told them sweetly that they could come back, they quickly returned; if I said nothing at all for a while, they would also come closer, but slowly. If I said "Go on then", they would immediately take a titbit. But with Star it often seemed as if she understood my meaning before I expressed it in voice or movement. She could read my facial expressions very well, just as well as my gestures and tone of voice. Her brain seemed to register my intentions even earlier than my own.

Star was friendly with the other Great Tits and was rather playful, certainly in her younger days. But she would not let the other birds boss her around: if she wanted to build a nest somewhere, she made sure that no one else came near, and that was also the case with her other projects.

In September and October the Great Tits always started their demolition work: tearing up paper and hammering holes in wood. They seemed to do this for pure delight. They had time to spare, because their youngsters could now look after themselves, and they had no need yet to prepare for the winter. In these games they displayed their own individual characters. There were some Great Tits who tore paper for fun and others who did it simply to attract the attention of another bird. Star was particularly zealous: her holes were deeper than those of the other Great Tits and she could tear paper more swiftly than anyone else. But at the end of November the birds always stopped this pastime, because it took them more time to find natural food and they had to prepare for winter.

1918

"Are you coming too?"

Thea is going to hand out suffragette pamphlets by the entrance of Holloway Gaol, because that's where they're force-feeding the women. She explains how they do it, with a tube in their throats and a funnel; it must be dreadful—two women have already died because it brought on pneumonia. I put my violin away, put on my coat. She pins a rosette to it.

When we're outside she links arms. "Peter's asked me to marry him. What do you think?" Sometimes she's just like a cat, round and purring.

"Do you love him?"

"Yes, quite a bit. I mean, not as much as Don. But enough maybe. And Don doesn't want to be tied down."

A rag-and-bone man drives past, straight through a puddle. The wheels of his cart spatter water against our legs. He's cursing and swearing at us—he must have seen the rosettes on our lapels.

"Don and you are exactly like each other."

"Yes, but that's precisely why it won't work. Music is enough for you, but I need someone who puts me first. To make me happy."

We change shifts with our fellow protesters at the square in front of the prison. "How did it go?" Thea asks.

"Boring. Just three men, and all of them prison officers. Can one of you p'raps give us a cig?"

Thea takes a case from her coat pocket and the girl helps herself to a cigarette. She shares it with her pal while they walk away, taking it in turns for a drag.

Thea asks if I'll come and have a meal with her later this week, when Peter will be there, so I can get to know him better and perhaps give her some advice. "I'm so impulsive. I mean, I do think I love him, but it's the same with all of them." An aeroplane drowns out her tale. We both look up.

Two soldiers are walking towards us. I recognise the one on the left. I think his name is Leo—he's one of the chaps Kingsley used to play tennis with, in Aberdovey. Perhaps he'll know something. I run towards him.

"Yes?" his friend says, frostily. We're allowed to protest here, but our presence isn't appreciated.

"Leo?"

His face brightens as he recognises me. "It's Gwen, isn't it?"

"Have you heard anything about Kingsley? We've heard nothing at all for a few months and most of the soldiers are back from France now, surely?"

A cloud passes overhead. "They haven't informed you?"

"What about?" Beneath my feet the ground gapes open in slow motion.

"The bombardment. The night before we were going to return. The whole camp was wiped out. We're not exactly sure who was there. Perhaps Kingsley was with the first detachment and he'd already left, but all the records were lost. Perhaps he's still in France, or on his way home. I was there too, but before Kingsley—so I don't know if he was there then or not."

Thea stands beside me and folds me into her arms.

"Kingsley is a strong, resourceful chap. It's quite possible that…" He looks directly at me. "It's chaos there. Perhaps he's in a hospital somewhere. Or he's making his own way home. No one knows exactly where they are and it's not very easy to get away. Men are still coming home."

Coming home, hope, hold on, get a grip, Kingsley. My father and Olive waved us off from the station in Wales; we shared a bar of chocolate in the train. His face, so familiar, a stranger, a soldier, I read, he gazes out of the window. France, a farm, hold on to hope. Thea talks to me, gives me a cigarette, I'm all light-headed.

"It can take weeks sometimes. One of my other mates got back just the day before yesterday. And it depends on how badly they're wounded." He turns to Thea. "No one's reported that things have gone badly for him."

"You should sit down a moment," Thea says. She towers above me, as my mother did before I fell asleep when I was little, as in those moments when my soul has almost let go of the day, grasps on to a few threads a little longer, and then yields.

*   *   *

The third time someone knocks at the door, I open it.

"Miss Howard. It's eleven o'clock already. I can't control what you do in your own time, but we can't keep breakfast waiting for you for ever." Mrs Sewell's face seems more deeply furrowed each week.

I nod. This afternoon we're starting to rehearse a new piece. I haven't practised it enough yet.

"Breakfast tomorrow will be at half past seven, as usual. If you wish for something else to eat today, then ask in the kitchen."

She turns around, thin and creased as crêpe paper. Her feet barely leave prints in the carpet.

I go and sit on the windowsill. The late autumn sun makes the chestnut treetops luminescent—yellow, ochre, red, redder. A stabbing in my belly, in my diaphragm—perhaps he'll never see this again. Thea kept insisting yesterday evening that we can't tell what's happened, that I mustn't lose heart. She said it again this morning. Don't lose heart, hope. He had no worries about the war, he wasn't the type to worry about anything. A good soldier, not made of granite but certainly of solid wood. But no one could really imagine how bad it was, not even when the first stories reached us from the trenches, when the first soldiers returned, when the newspapers wrote reports—now we have photographs too.

A military truck drives past in the street below, tooting its horn, and there's a group of children at the roadside, cheering. A soldier walks past them, arm in arm with a nurse. Her laughter cuts off my breath.

My dress is draped over the foot of my bed. The fabric feels cold for a moment, and then takes on the temperature of my skin.

The banister rail gives some support. It's colder outside than it seemed, so I go back for a warmer coat and my soft velvet bonnet, and try again. When the door slams shut behind me, it makes me jump. But it's only on reaching the rehearsal room that I realise I've forgotten my violin. Stockdale lets

Joan take me home. "We really don't need you this week. Just make sure that you practise every day. It'll do you good. Chin up." He pats a little colour into my cheek.

*   *   *

"Gwen, we must go now. We're already late." Thea is at the open door. "Come on, darling. I know you're not in the mood. But you can't let the children down. Truly."

She takes my hand and tugs me up. I grasp my violin case and follow her downstairs, out of the front door, out of the street, to Don's house. He's started a little school for the children in his neighbourhood. They have classes twice a week, violin and piano. Thea helps Don with the piano classes, I help with the violin. They're too small still for the cello. He has a rich uncle who has bought some second-hand violins for him, and some of the orchestra have donated old instruments.

One of the youngest children, Paulie, is standing at the door waiting for us. "Thea!" He throws his arms around her waist and presses his filthy little body against hers.

"Clever boy—you're here already!" She asks if his sister is here too. He doesn't know, scratches a scab off his cheek; the black dirt from his nails remains in the wound. His pals run into the street, yelling; the smallest boy falls over, seems to want to cry for a moment, then swiftly races towards us with the others.

There are twelve children in all. We put them in a circle and start warming up. We always begin with a little song. "Happy or sad?" "Happy," half of them shout. "Sad," the other half cry. For a few minutes it casts its spell on them. After that they're allowed to play. We're halfway through 'Frère Jacques' now. Michael is concentrating so hard that his tongue sticks out. Paulie is distracted and is running around. Thea sits him down again, with his violin. The girls are really doing their best. Bert and Timmy are always laughing. Once a week isn't enough. They have no other stimulus. These children aren't from the worst families: they have shoes; their teeth are mostly white, not black; they're not as thin as the street urchins who live behind Mrs Sewell's house. But they all have too many brothers and sisters and only Paulie and Timmy regularly go to school.

Timmy is the first one to get it right. *Frère Jacques, Frère Jacques, dormez-vous?* The other children clap in time for him, and he has to play it again, for the group now. His eyes shine; he licks his lips and plays it one more time, almost perfectly. The other children stand up to clap and he moves his shoulders up and down, full of bottled-up pride. Thea praises him, and I do too, and then we carry on with the lesson, going back to basics, for the other children. Timmy plays along, very seriously now; he's no longer fooling around with Bert.

On the other side of the window grey shifts into grey: stone, street, smoke. I must keep on watching the children.

When the lesson is over, I put on my coat.

"Aren't you going to stay for tea?" Thea is in the little kitchen. "Don will be home soon."

I shake my head. "Sorry."

She takes hold of me and presses me to her for a moment. "Look after yourself, won't you? I'll see you later."

Timmy runs towards me when I'm at the door and flings his arms round me. "Can I come with you?" I kiss his head and say we'll see each other soon.

I walk through the garden to the back street, then into the next alley. Stone on stone. My feet sound louder than is pleasant. I know that the back street is always the same width and isn't narrower today than on other days, but it feels so. Before I reach the shopping street I can hear already how busy it is—people, carts, buses, carriages, everyone moving through each other—I quicken my pace, simply looking ahead, that is quite enough, more than enough. Two men with umbrellas—I only realise that it's raining when I see them—a woman holding a child's hand, another child in her wake, a horse and cart on the other side of the road. Bang. I turn round and see a Pigeon wing fluttering, walk back to it—the other wing is broken, its abdomen torn open, the Pigeon is still alive, looking at me from one eye, she can't move her head—this Pigeon is going to die, there's really nothing to be done—I look around, there's a pile of bricks against one of the houses a little further on, I can't see any other option, so I take a brick, meanwhile everyone simply walks on, no one has noticed the Pigeon, carts drive back and forth, coachmen guide their horses just past it—I must hurry, that poor creature, the Pigeon looks at me again when I return, sorry, I say, I'm terribly sorry, and I kneel down and slam the brick onto the Pigeon as hard as I can, smash the skull to pieces in a single blow, and I strike again although the Pigeon is already dead, the Pigeon is now truly dead—I stand up and put the brick back on the pile against the wall, blood making small feathers stick to its underside, another Pigeon is watching some way off, its mate, probably, and I whisper sorry once again and then I walk on and people are still acting as if they haven't seen anything at all, though there really was something to see, and now I'm probably weeping but it's raining and so my tears can't be seen, and no one looks closely enough anyway.

*　　　*　　　*

I wake up at half past four for the fourth morning in succession. I listen to the city, almost silent at this hour. Every morning voices swell up, die down after a few hours, then grow louder as the afternoon progresses, only to die down further as the evening comes to a close, whispering the night in. The wind moves the windows and the curtains, branches, leaves. Houses keep the wind outside, let laughter in. Footsteps make the street speak. Horses' hooves mark time. Motor engines lay low bass notes under the sound of wheels on stone. I make sounds too. At night I can hear myself: breath, heart, thoughts. I miss the sea, the fields of my childhood, the silence that the Blackbirds let you hear. The past: that which means you're here now. No: the past is a hill in the distance which can never come closer, but which can also never really recede. Now is a face in the crowds that suddenly gains expression, that looks back at you, passes you by.

Olive has written to say that Kingsley has perhaps started a new life in France, that he's met a girl there. That seems like a tall story to me—he hasn't any reason not to get in touch with us, and although letters might take a long time to reach home they are arriving again. The army hasn't yet responded to our enquiries. I last saw him a week before he left for France, in the pub. Thea was there too. They'd just heard they were sending them to the Front, but Kingsley was no different than usual. Serene. Margie was in France too. He was going to get in touch with her, if he had the chance. There was drinking and lively tales—about the girls there, and the drink, and battles that failed to come. They sang popular songs, which everyone could sing along to, except me, which made Kingsley and his pals laugh out loud, seeing that I was the musician. After that evening there were just two letters home, to my parents.

My eyes are smarting. I'd better go for a walk. I quietly get dressed, open the door, pad across the velvety carpet down the stairs—my feet know the stair treads, know how big a step they must take.

I walk towards the Thames through the darkness. In the shopping street I see a tramp and two streets further on a group of washerwomen. No one else is around at all. In the distance I can hear a Blackbird. He calls differently to the Blackbirds at home. Three gliding notes, a trill at the end. I hum the tune back. Next time I must bring a pencil and paper with me. A second Blackbird sings the answer. I scan the trees. The first one repeats its song. I can hear where the sound is coming from, but I can't see the birds. They fall silent, I walk on. Tomorrow I'll come again, and then I'll bring a notebook with me.

*　　　*　　　*

"Brahms's First Symphony." Stockdale is giving out the parts. "Gwen, in the second movement you'll play principal violin."

Billie smiles at me, shifts to one side. She gives my leg a little pat as I sit down.

I blush. I've played solo previously, in a Mozart piece, but then two days before the premiere Stockdale gave my part to Davey, because I wasn't yet ready for it.

"It'll be fine," Billie whispers.

We have to start the piece three times over because the tempo isn't correct. I can feel my heartbeat quicken as we get close to the solo, and play softer than usual, too soft, see Billie glance at me, wrestle my way through the notes—what I'm playing is right, but it simply has no meaning. We play the piece again, and again, and then Stockdale sends us home. "I take it that everyone understands what the homework is? Gwen, will you stay behind for a moment?"

I pack away my violin, daren't look at him directly.

"Sit down." With a flamboyant gesture he points to the chair beside him.

"It was awful, wasn't it?"

He waves the words away. "It'll be all right. As long as you practise. Do you think you'll manage that?"

"I have practised."

"I realise that, but I mean that you'll have to work harder, really hard. And I think that's the best thing for you. But we don't have to do this. I can easily give the solo to Billie."

I shake my head. "I can do it."

"Good." He gives me a pat. "I think your parents will want to be at the premiere."

That night there are coloured rings around the full moon. A glory, Kingsley once told me.

*   *   *

Two weeks later I go to Wales for a long weekend. Olive wrote that Mother doesn't want to leave her bed and Father's doing nothing at all about it. My shoes feel like lead that morning and my feet too. It's not the right time to return.

"The Lost Sheep!" My father is waiting at the station in his best suit. The lines by his mouth are deeper when he smiles at me; there are thick grey hairs in his bushy eyebrows. He kisses my cheek and picks up my heavy suitcase. On the way home I tell him about the orchestra, about my solo, about the Magpie I found last spring, which I kept in a box for a few weeks, before setting it free again. When I ask him about his poems he says they're still worthless, that he can't quite put his finger on what's wrong. We walk over a carpet of leaves, mud in the centre, borders shifted by the wind. When we reach the houses, we stop talking.

The house is smaller than I remember; paint is peeling off the window frames. There's a wreath on the front door, evergreen branches braided with red ribbons. Cook opens the door and embraces me. "My dear. I'm so pleased to see you." She pushes me away from her to take a good look at me, and then draws me close again. "You're a proper young lady now. And how is your fiddle playing?"

"Sis." Olive is coming down the stairs. "Good to see you home at last." She's wearing a long grey dress. There's a faint blueness round her eyes, but I can't tell if she's wearing eye shadow or if it's the colour of her skin. She kisses my left cheek. No perfume, just the smell of old paper.

My father hands Cook my suitcase. "Dudley has his study in your old bedroom. Cook has made up the guest room for you."

"Tea is in an hour's time," Olive says. "Perhaps you could ask Mother if she'll join us."

I follow Cook upstairs, hesitating on the last few steps. The door to my mother's room is ajar. Cook keeps walking, and on the second flight calls out again that she's so pleased I'm home. "Me too," I say. I knock, and then open the door.

The room is in semi-darkness. I walk to the window, push the curtains aside a little and then open the top window—fresh air will do her good. My mother is sitting straight up in bed, with pillows behind her back. She's wearing a dressing gown over her nightdress. "Gwennie. Come here and give your mother a kiss."

I sit on the edge of her bed and allow myself to be embraced—perfume, cigarettes, the smell of sleep. On her night table there's a cup of tea, half a sandwich, an ashtray. Beside the plate there's a pile of letters.

"It's so awful, Gwen. When I got your letter, I knew immediately that there was something wrong. I had heart trouble already, you know, I wrote to you about that, and now the problem has started all over again." She holds her breast. "Here." She speaks about Dudley, says that Kingsley is really the second son she's lost.

My leg has gone to sleep. I change position. "Will you come down for tea?"

She smiles. "Can you close the window, darling? I can't bear the draught."

"Mother, I asked you a question."

She stares at me, then with her left hand sketches a horizon in the air. "You mustn't think you can simply come here and boss me around."

"I was just asking you something."

"Oh, just asking me something."

I stand up, close the window, move to the door. "Till later, then."

On the first floor, I enter my old room. The bookshelves are empty. My bird books are nowhere to be seen.

We wait a quarter of an hour. "Let's start," my father says. He helps himself to a sandwich, and takes a bite, swallowing it without chewing.

"I'll go upstairs, then." Olive fiercely pushes her chair back.

Dudley takes a scone from the serving plate.

"Do you play music still?" I ask him. He used to play the cello.

"No." He shoves the scone into his mouth.

"What a shame."

Olive returns, shakes her head. My father leaves, making his way to his bedroom. When he's out of earshot, Olive leans towards me. "There are stories going round that they're not dead, but were sent to a camp. That they'll be back soon. But don't tell Mother and Father. I don't want to give them false hopes."

"How do you know?"

"Margie wrote to me. One of her friends was a soldier there."

"Kingsley would write to us if he got the chance, surely?"

"Perhaps he's wounded." Olive swallows. The corner of her mouth curls up for a moment. "Or he's confused."

"Perhaps he just doesn't want to come back." Dudley puts his fork down. "That's something I can picture. That he prefers it like it is. Nice and peaceful."

We both stare at him.

"I'd jolly well like that too." He takes a large gulp of milk; drops slide down his chin, fall onto his collar. "Nice bit of sunshine, jolly little drink, nice bit of cheese."

"I don't think he's had much time for jolly little drinks and nice bits of cheese," I say.

Dudley wipes the milk from his chin with his cuff, then shrugs his shoulders. "I can well imagine it. After all, he won't get any money now."

Olive looks startled.

"What do you mean?" I frown at him.

"Haven't they told you yet?" Dudley laughs. "Those who leave home won't get a thing."

I wipe my mouth on my napkin and go upstairs. I knock three times.

"Yes?" My father doesn't turn.

"Will you come bird-watching? We can walk to the woods or the beach. Just a short stroll."

"Sorry. I want to finish this." He takes off his spectacles and polishes the lenses with a handkerchief.

"Does Charles still come by sometimes?"

"Charles?" He puts on his glasses and turns towards me.

"Oh, come on, Papa. The Crow!"

"Oh yes, of course. I haven't seen him for some time now. I did spot him last year, I believe. He came less and less, though, once you were gone." He coughs. "Was there anything else?"

I walk to the woods along the path behind the house, then through the fields to the beach. Charles is nowhere to be seen. He should be alive still—he wasn't all that old. Perhaps he's just gone away. Perhaps he's angry with me and that's why he won't show himself. He could be anywhere. There's no point in carrying on searching. On the beach a fine rain draws grey stripes in the air—grey sand, grey sea, grey sky. My lips are salty. I hum out notes to hear my voice—they blow away.

Mother doesn't come downstairs at all during the weekend.

"Goodbye, Mama." I lean down, kiss her cheek.

"So you're going away from us again." She turns away from me.

"The train leaves in two hours. I still have to pack. Olive is coming to the station with me."

"You've done your duty. Visiting your old mother."

"I wanted to see you all."

"You haven't come home for four years."

"And none of you have come to London either." I take a deep breath and try to make my voice sound friendlier. "In a couple of weeks we'll hold the premiere of our new piece, and I have a solo. Would you all like to come? There's a good hotel near the concert hall. Stockdale would appreciate it too."

She looks at me a moment, then smiles. "Would you close the door properly when you leave? There's such a terrible draught in here."

Olive writes, some months later, to let me know that she's heard from Kingsley. He said in his letter that he was sorry he hadn't written earlier, that he'd met a young woman, that he has a son now, called Jacques after her father, that he works in a butcher's shop with his father-in-law, somewhere in the north of France, that he'll stay there for the foreseeable future, that he'll write again soon, that he hopes to see us before long, that he has to save up for a visit, that he hopes all is well, that it's beautiful where he lives, long fields with sunflowers and hills and a sun that's warmer and yellower than here.

STAR 6

My friend Garth Christian, a naturalist who also writes about bird behaviour, sent me an article about an experiment on Jackdaws, which showed that they could learn to count. "Can your birds do this too?" he had written above it. That set me thinking. Star did not roost inside the house, yet at six o'clock every morning she was the first to arrive for a nut. The next morning, when she was at the windowsill again, I decided to try it out.

"No," I said to her. "First, you have to tap." I looked into her eyes and said very clearly: "Tap. Tap." I tapped my knuckles on the wood. Star tapped her beak twice against the window frame. Then she flew to my hand for her nut. I knew that Star was intelligent, but I had not expected this—she knew exactly what I wanted! It made me think of Twist, another very unusual Great Tit, who would give me a kiss if I asked her. The next day I again asked Star to tap, and once more she did what I requested. We repeated the experiment another four times that day, and each time she tapped back.

The next day there was a problem. Star flew into the house, tapped on the wood three times, and flew to my hand for her nut. I did not give her it because I wanted her to imitate my tapping—after all, I was teaching her to count. So then she flew off, quite offended. By her standards she stayed away for rather a long time afterwards, four hours at least, and on returning she again tapped three times on the window frame. So then I gave her the nut she wanted, because she clearly thought she had done something well and I did not wish to offend her anew. The next time, fortunately, she waited for my instructions.

The following step was to teach her how to tap out the correct numbers. If I tapped twice, she had to tap twice in response, and only then would she receive her nut. She swiftly understood. Tapping two was successful, three too, but when I gave four taps she looked doubtfully at me, as if she could not hear them well. I was tapping with my knuckles on wood. Perhaps that sound was too dark and muffled. I then tried with a pencil and that worked very well. We practised in that manner during the following weeks: four, five, six and then seven taps. She tapped the larger numbers in groups of two, three and four. Eight, for example, was tapped as two groups of four, very occasionally as three-three-two. Star usually cooperated extremely well, and often wanted to tap of her own accord, although there were also some mornings when she could not be persuaded. If she felt like tapping, then she would perch on the edge of the window, her head pointing at her feet; if she did not wish to do it, she held her beak in the air. She obviously found it fun, but only in the right circumstances, and I did not always understand what those were.

In February the lessons were interrupted because the territorial war had broken out again. Baldhead was too weak to do battle and Star took on both Smoke and Inkey. Females rarely fight with males. I had never witnessed it before and never saw it again. During this period, if I tapped for Star, she simply gave me a sidelong glance, and if I did not offer her a nut, she would hammer on the wood until I gave in. A few times, when there was a lull in the squabbles, we had a couple of tapping sessions, but Star had her mind on other matters.

1921

We're sitting in a semicircle with the first violins, twenty-eight legs in dark trousers and stockings. "More expression," Stockdale snaps at Joan, who nervously lowers her eyes. "And a strict one, two, three. Stress on the one." We've started the piece thirteen times already and each time something is wrong. But the problem lies with Stockdale himself, who keeps changing the tempo—this time it's faster—as if his mind isn't quite on the task. "All together," Stockdale says. We start on the upbeat. I close my eyes and let myself be carried along by the cellist beside me. He's always just a little too quick, a fraction, so if I play a little slower, then it's right. "No, no, stop." Stockdale shakes his head. "That's enough. We'll resume tomorrow. Joan, I really expect more feeling, more energy. I don't want it louder but fuller. If you continue like this, I think we won't be able to carry on together."

Joan has tears in her eyes. She rubs at her gaunt cheeks, making them more hollow.

"Don't take any notice of him," I say when Stockdale has gone. "His uncertainty is affecting your performance." Not just her performance, but her whole self, as if she were his echo. I put my violin in its case. It's not performing that irritates me, never, it's the people.

Priscilla is in a rush, is suddenly there in front of me when I stand. She stumbles. "Oh God, sorry," she says to her cello.

Joan walks outside with me. "It's always like this," she says. "I clam up if someone treats me that way. Even now. Even though I've known Stockdale so long, know exactly what he's like."

"I understand." Stockdale blew his top last week and sacked yet another clarinettist.

It's October. Leaves are blowing against the window. A young, red-haired chap stands in front of the Art School, smoking. I walk past him with Joan. He says hallo. I say hallo back to him.

"Hang on a mo." He stubs out his cigarette. "Can I ask you something, or are you in a hurry?" I stand still, my head cocked, like a Blackbird's. Joan says she has to go and she'll see me tomorrow.

The young man is often here and we've been greeting each other for several weeks now. He looks at me, but says nothing. "I can't wait all day, you know," I say, taking a step towards the spindly birch trees further along.

He shakes his head. "Shall we go for a walk then?" A yellow leaf blows against him. "Or a coffee?" He takes the leaf from his forehead and carefully examines it for a moment. The clouds above us mirror the whole world, each and every thing.

In a café by the Thames he shows me his drawings. Birds, horses, dogs, fabulous creatures, lines that flow into their surroundings, that not only make me see him differently when I look up again, but everything else too.

"They're just sketches," he says.

I pick out the Jackdaw he showed me, and tell him about Nora, the Jackdaw I reared, who stayed with me for three whole years. "After the first year she'd sometimes go exploring, but she always stayed in the neighbourhood. Last year, in the spring, she suddenly vanished. I think she must have met someone, or else she found a good place to nest. Jackdaws have minds of their own, you know." I take a sip of coffee. "I found her near Hyde Park when she was just a few weeks old. The parents were nowhere to be seen. Baby Jackdaws learn to fly from the ground, you see, so you mustn't simply take them away if you find one." Some people have never held a bird—those soft feathers, that vulnerability, so much life in something so small.

Outside the gale is increasing. Long grey lines move across the water, all equally grey; drops become larger drops become a river; what the wind blows upwards changes back into rain.

"I thought I'd be happy here, that it would just happen. Away from my parents, away from what was expected, alone with my violin."

"So you aren't happy, then?"

"When I play, I'm happy." The orchestra stifles me sometimes. Joan and Billie keep asking if I'll go dancing with them, when I'd rather be out of doors in my free time. I have another pile of notebooks now, filled with bird stories.

"Come on then, let's go. The wind is wonderful outside."

He pushes the door open, into the wind, gives me his arm. I close my eyes and smell the river, autumn, the future. He holds his sketches under his coat to protect them from the rain. And we walk like this to Vauxhall, into the approaching evening, as the lamps are lit inside the houses, as a Robin hides himself within the greenness that will be here a little longer still.

*　　　*　　　*

His face is with me the whole weekend, and the lilt of his voice—I can't hear its precise tone any more; I only know how he spoke the words, drawing them out just a bit. When I'm bringing a stack of bird books back to the library, I twice think I see him. My surroundings turn into a screen onto which he's projected. Thomas. Thea whistled when I told her about him. She said it was high time I lost control of myself a little.

On Monday, when the rehearsal is over, I'm the first to pack my violin, the first at the door. He isn't there. I wait. Pigeons are keeping an eye on the street from the roof across the road. When the last of the wind section comes out, I pretend I've forgotten something. I walk back through the stream of chitchat. There are still people in the room. I go to the lavatory, lock the door, wait, then slowly walk outside again, stopping to chat with Stockdale at the front door. He was satisfied today and thinks that the premiere on Friday will go splendidly. Thomas isn't there, I can't go inside again, so I walk home and try to remember if he was ever there before on a Monday.

On Tuesday we rehearse later. I look out for him before going in, and again during the break, then take my time packing up. I talk to Billie, help Stockdale think about a change of tempo, listen to the new cellist who is explaining something to Joan about vibrato—he's all aglow, this skinny, lopsided man who suddenly has two women hanging on his words. I can still see Thomas's face before me, wish for him to be waiting outside; he knows when I'll finish. "Ladies, gentleman, this is all very interesting about the cello, but now we must stop." Stockdale raises his hands to thrust us out of the room. "Off you go." I daren't look, keep my eyes fixed on the door, can't spot anyone in front of the building. I linger near the doorway.

Behind us two Sparrows fly into a hedge. Their wings are so swift that I can't see them move. "Look," I say, pointing at the hedge.

Billie gives me a questioning look. "Coming for a drink?"

"Sorry. Prior engagement."

They vanish into the street, their voices dying away, drowned out by horses, wheels, wagons, other people. So many others.

I wait till the clock strikes five, hopeful as a puppy dog, and then walk home. All the time I'm walking, I expect him to come up behind me. I listen for him without glancing back. I'd hear his voice above the wind, the wind would help me.

Wednesday, Thursday. My body has never felt so untouched before.

On Friday we have the final rehearsal. The sky is clear, the sun makes the leaves on the ground look an even deeper yellow. Ochre. I feel calmer, no longer so full of him. The rehearsal goes well. We have to be at the concert hall by seven o'clock; Stockdale suggests we should go out together for a bite to eat. I leave the building with Priscilla, and then, after all, there he is. "Hang on."

I run to the other side of the street.

"Hallo, Gwen. I've got something for you. And it's nice walking weather. Shall we go to the park?"

I gesture towards the other members of the orchestra. "We're off to eat somewhere. It's the premiere tonight."

He takes a small packet from his satchel, presses it into my hands. "Where will the performance be?"

I tell him the address. "And now I really have to go. What's in it?"

"A surprise." He touches my shoulder, turns round and walks away.

"He'll come to the performance tonight," I announce to Joan, because I have to tell someone.

"Wonderful," she says. "Let's hope it all goes well." Joan often throws up before a performance—her passion for the violin barely outweighs her fear.

I can't spot him in the auditorium, but I play as if he's there. The piece we're performing is like a landscape: at first there's grass (and each blade of grass is alive), then water—a river that turns brackish and then joins the sea; there is water all the time, in fact, sometimes calm, sometimes swirling—then a line, a horizon or a coast, a still frame around all the movement, a fence in front of a transition that is both unexpected and expected; the landscape changes, becomes hilly, steep cliffs, rocks, depths, firm ground in the distance, mountains in the distance, and from the mountains you can see everything, or nearly everything, and you think you can see everything that exists, the whole world, and when you come down again it's clear that it's all endlessly intricate and detailed and complex, far more than you thought, and that what is in the smallest things is also in the largest: you're here now, you've been everywhere and you've never left your spot.

Playing is like flying: the altitude, speed, lightness, the confidence that the magic will endure, that the magic can be trusted, for as long as it lasts. Playing, the word says it all. We play. And through our playing we enable those on the ground to see something, those gazing awestruck through their telescopes, those who can never view the world from above, except on the rare occasions they're carried by someone else.

At the end of the performance Stockdale thanks me, his face warm, the muscles relaxed—he's handsome when he's like that, and I can see why they all fall for him. "Finally, it went as it should. I was afraid we were going to founder." His shirt is damp beneath his evening suit. It sticks to his skin.

"You shouldn't be so nervy." I put my violin in its case.

He shakes his head. "If nothing is at stake, then nothing happens. I have to make you feel what it's all about."

"If you tighten a string too much, it will snap."

"But strings can take a lot of tightening. Are you coming with us?" His breath is warm against my cheek.

I say no, thanks. I long for a place with no voices.

The moon is full, the second time this month, so it's a blue moon. I tuck the violin case firmly under my arm and walk through streets that seem emptier than usual, walking slowly because I feel at home within this walking, within what passes by.

I find the little packet again only the next morning. It's a drawing, on brown paper, of a Great Tit. The little creature is looking at me just as Thomas does. I hang it above my music stand, next to the window.

*   *   *

"This is my home." Thomas swings open the red door of the houseboat, bends down and enters ahead of me. "Like a cup of tea?"

At the front of the cabin there is a small kitchen. There's a large painting on the worktop—red sun, water, reflections, colours. "How lovely!"

"Oh, that. It isn't finished yet. The colours are fine but the composition's awful." He searches in the little cupboards, then turns around, as if he has suddenly thought of something, and takes my hand. The boat is lifted up by a wave. "I'm so pleased you're here."

In the weeks that follow I get to know the river through the movements of the boat. I become familiar with the Swans who live a little further on with their four large children and who regularly glide past the round porthole above the bed, the bed below the waterline. I become familiar with the light that makes the water glitter and with the mist that makes the waves fade into the distance. The water that makes the sheets damp in the morning, makes the wooden planks warp. And I become acquainted with the Great Tits who nest on the ledge above the door, with the soft sloshing of the water, signals from a muted world.

I bring my violin with me and play for him; when we're in bed together I read him my bird notes. There are tall trees on the quayside, with shrubs between, and if I wake up early in the morning I often go and sit on deck to listen and look. It's not as loud here as in the city. I can hear myself think.

Thomas touches me, again and again, and when I walk through the city, when I play the violin, when I talk to others, it happens afresh, my body suddenly remembers things that make me redden. The body has its own memory, its own ideas about what is important.

"My compliments," Stockdale says after the first concert when Thomas is in the audience. "You're really hitting the nail on the head now."

Thomas is waiting for me at the door. He's smoking a cigarette, looking towards the end of the street, tapping the fingers of his empty hand against his trousers. I stay watching him like that a moment, then open the door. He laughs, drops his cigarette, takes my face in his hands. "Beautiful," he says and suddenly I doubt that he means it, that he actually means everything that's happened, that I mean it too. I thank him and see myself standing there, not young any more, and certainly not promising, and only when he kisses me is this feeling broken, and I see him again.

*   *   *

In November Olive comes to London. She's staying with me. Mrs Sewell has made up the guest room for her. I see her standing in the crowds in Waterloo Station, looking nervously from left to right, like a Crested Grebe. "Olive!" I raise my hand; she searches, spots me. "Over here." She smells just the same as when I last saw her. I take her suitcase from her. "It's a fifteen-minute walk. Are you tired? Do you want to take the bus?"

"I'm happy to walk. I've been sitting for the whole journey." She gives my face a sidelong glance. "You look marvellous, Gwen. Are things going well for you?"

I feel caught out, mutter that everything's all right.

She doesn't notice, or doesn't let me see she's noticed. I tell her about the city, the streets, the houses, the busyness, the orchestra and the new pieces we're playing. She is smaller than I remember, more fragile, and her voice seems softer. "How are Papa and Mama?"

"Not too bad. Papa has finally finished his collection about the war. And he's back to his usual self, meddling in everything. Mama is just the same as ever." She looks sidelong at me. "It upsets her that you hardly ever write."

"But she's always reproaching me."

"You shouldn't have left home then."

I shake my head. The irritation I haven't felt for years is suddenly back again, in full force. I take a deep breath. After all, it's not Olive's fault.

"What about you?"

She shrugs her shoulders, looks away.

"Olive. Are you in love?"

"Perhaps." We cross the road. She tags behind, as if I'm the leader.

"What's his name?"

"Timothy." She takes a deep breath. "He's fifty. And he's married."

"Oh, that's a shame."

"His wife is ill. Mental problems. She's in a special ward at the hospital. I met him there, when I went with Dud for his physical therapy."

"Does he love you too?"

"It doesn't matter, Gwen. I shouldn't have said anything."

That evening she comes to the premiere of Beethoven's Ninth. When the concert is over we go to the hotel bar with the others.

"It's so good to see you here at last." Stockdale is standing too close to Olive, who sidesteps away from him till she's standing by the wall. "Both the Howard sisters. Together again, finally." He gives her hand another kiss. "How are your parents?"

"Very well. Father has just finished his new collection."

"It will be worth the wait." He drains his whisky in a single draught. "I've rarely read such an original poet. He has not achieved the fame he deserves, but posterity will judge differently."

Olive is drinking sherry, greedily, like my mother. Someone taps my shoulder.

"Len." A kiss.

"Thomas. This is my sister, Olive." His hand is on my arm.

"Pleased to meet you." He kisses her hand. "This is Stella."

A blonde girl in a black velvet dress, no older than twenty, steps out from behind him. Her eyes are lined with kohl. She laughs like an actress.

"And who is Stella?" I ask.

"We've just met each other." He laughs apologetically. "She's studying at the Art School, too. Sculpture."

I search his face for an explanation, and, when I can't find one, for a reason.

"Anyone for another drink?" He laughs a little, cheerful, frank, nothing the matter at all.

As he's standing at the bar, Olive leans towards me. "Is that him?" she whispers.

I nod.

"Who's the girl?"

"No idea." A girl, one of the many girls whose existence I knew of, or suspected, and suspecting is different to seeing.

Olive scowls. I pick up my glass from the table and take a large gulp. The champagne tastes sour, although no one else has said anything, so perhaps it's something to do with me.

Stockdale holds out his hand and Olive steps onto the dance floor. She moves her body just a little too fast. Stockdale lags a fraction behind, tries to shift her into the right rhythm. They make a jerky couple.

Olive is in high spirits on the way home, and more open than usual. She links arms with me. "Sore feet. Pretty shoes, but no good for walking." She's wearing my new high heels—I can't play if my feet aren't flat on the ground. "That chap, Thomas. Awfully good-looking. Are you in love with him?"

"Yes." It's too dark to see her face; the moonlight falls over her ear. She doesn't probe further. "It's different here," I say. We're walking along the Thames, we'll turn left before we reach his boat. "Thea, the cellist, you know, has already had five boyfriends. Only Priscilla is married. But even she had an affair with a trumpet player, before I joined the orchestra." But Patricia is married. Perhaps she's had children by now.

"But is it him who doesn't want to marry, or you?"

"Neither of us wants it, I suppose." We look carefully before we cross the road, even though it's night now, and there's no traffic. Like children, cautious in a city so much bigger than they are, that doesn't care about them at all.

"Anyway, congratulations." She laughs. "He's much handsomer than Paul, remember?"

I don't tell her she's drunk, and join in her laughter a little. The pavement is uneven and I keep a tight hold on her, otherwise she'll fall, with those heels on. Olive tells me about Timothy, that his wife will perhaps die soon, that it would be awful, of course, and yet she still hopes it will happen—her voice is as comforting as the sound of the sea. I try to follow what she's saying, but my thoughts keep prowling in the region between what actually is and what might happen.

*   *   *

"So what exactly is going on with you and that girl?"

"You're not jealous, hey? I thought we'd agreed we wouldn't be jealous?" He puts his rinsed brushes back in the jar, with a little more force than necessary.

"I'm only asking." Letting someone in means letting something go, means letting yourself go. It doesn't mean clinging, or hoping. To desire someone always means you have to let them go, because there's always a space that doesn't belong to you, a space inside the other person, where you can't be. It also means being able to lose someone and accepting that, because something exists that's more important than anything else. According to him, at least.

"I met her by chance and we had a drink together and then danced. You were the one who said to take things slowly."

"I'm only asking." I smile to show him I'm not cross, but I don't manage to make my smile quite cheerful or friendly enough.

"Gwen, you know what I'm like."

I don't really know, but I'm pleased he says so. As if he isn't hiding anything from me. Honesty is important. And I don't want to marry. I want to play the violin and travel. I want to move. He understands what it means to move, and perhaps this is what movement costs. I don't know why my throat is tight, why swallowing doesn't help.

He takes a step towards me, folds his wet fingers over mine. "Come on then, we'll go to the museum."

My coat feels rough and familiar, my black hat too. We walk beside the water to the bus stop. There's a Heron in the reeds, grey as the water. In the oak by the corner there are two Crows. Thomas talks and laughs and shows me the colours of things, the words people use, the half-trampled bouquet of flowers in the gutter, the shadow that a policeman casts over the street, the long body.

His long body. I can hear his voice in my head, its sound, its timbre, its intonation. His body is still always new. This morning he started out, knowing precisely how and where (my shoulder, innocently, my arm, my hand, my shoulder again, my neck, a kiss, skin, gentle brushing, lips, opening). So precisely that I sometimes ask myself if he's touching me, or just a woman.

In the museum he walks like a slow skater, his hands on his back: part child, part philosopher. He makes me see the paintings afresh. Paint, mood, colour, colour, colour. When we reach Turner, he takes my hand. We stand still and look, and I can see what has touched him. He was right—I do know what he's like.

STAR 7

Star always devoted a great deal of time to rearing her young. She brought them food far longer than most Tits do and taught them various useful skills. One of the things she taught her children each year was that there was no need to be afraid of me. They passed this on to their own children, and so I was the friend not only of particular individuals, but of specific families too.

One of the sons from Star and Baldhead's first brood was an unusually fine-looking bird. Everyone who saw him said: "What a beauty!" And so I called him Beauty. Beauty was the first to follow his mother from the nest to the bird table, and he kept visiting it long after he had fledged. He always carefully considered which nuts to choose. Most Great Tits take several titbits from the table and only decide if they will eat something after they have already taken it; Beauty always considered it in advance and never chose something he would not then eat. He remained in the garden until he was four months old, and then left with three other young birds. I did not see them for a long time afterwards and was afraid that something had happened, but after three months I suddenly saw him on the windowsill, the other three in his wake.

The following spring he nested in my garden with a scraggy female called Dolly. His territory bordered on his mother's. Dolly and Beauty had a large brood and worked hard to give all their chicks sufficient food. The last one to fly the nest, a little female, had a lame leg. I called her Naomi. He brought her to me when she was ten days old; she trusted me immediately because he did. Naomi was slower than the others and

I fed her until she had gained the skill to search out food for herself. After a few months she was able to use her leg a little better, and after a year you could barely see that it had previously troubled her so greatly. She no longer needed my help and was just as independent as the other Great Tits.

1937

The sun is already hot, one Tuesday morning in May, as I'm on my way to Mr Taylor the solicitor's office. Blackbirds are nesting in the high hedge at the corner of the street. They're flying back and forth with food for their young, but the spot that they've chosen is really not appropriate. It's far too exposed, an easy target for cats and Magpies. I unbutton my jacket—I'm wearing a dark-blue woollen suit and am already starting to perspire. I've brought my violin with me because I have to rehearse immediately after this appointment. The handle of the case slips in my damp hand at each step, forwards, backwards. I strengthen my grip and suck my tongue to help me swallow.

I'm five minutes early but I knock three times on the door with the heavy knocker. I follow the maid through a large marble hallway into an office. Mother would certainly adore this house. "Mr Taylor will be with you soon," the maid says. I put my violin case down beside my chair, where it immediately falls over. I really should have asked for a glass of water.

"Miss Howard." A stocky little man with a moustache and small round spectacles approaches me, his hand thrust out. "Good to see you." He sits down at his desk and opens a folder of papers. "First, of course, my condolences for your loss. I met your father once or twice, we had friends in common. He was a most amiable man with a vast knowledge of poetry."

"Yes, indeed." I try to swallow.

"Would you like some water?" He stands up and calls the maid, who then brings me a glass. "I can imagine that it came as a shock to you, even though he was ill."

I nod. I didn't know he was ill; I hadn't been home for years. I sent my parents postcards when I was on holiday, and cards at Christmas, and sometimes I'd write a letter to Olive. I have no idea why Olive only wrote about it after the funeral, in November last year—she said she'd been busy, and that Mother hadn't wanted me to come. I sent them a stone bird, to put on his grave.

"Mr Howard has left all his assets and property to his four children." My heart is thudding. My share is much greater than I expected—I could buy a small house with it. Mother will be furious.

I sign the paper to accept my inheritance and within ten minutes I'm outside again, where the light is so intense that I can't see anything for a moment.

*   *   *

"Joan, start again."

"Sorry, *why* do I have to start again?" The muscle by her mouth is twitching worse than ever. Her face is only calm when she's playing.

"You're the one who has to set the tempo for the others. Guide. Lead. But instead you first follow the violins, and then the bass."

She nods, without looking up from her violin.

"Again." Joan begins and we follow, three bars later. Through the window, high up behind her, I can see a Crow flying.

"Utter rubbish. Stop. We'll start the second part."

Suddenly he's there in front of me, making me jump. "Gwendolen. Are you with us?"

A few days ago I saw a Crow drop a twig while flying. Another Crow caught it, flew up, also dropped it, and the first one swooped down, just in time to catch the twig again. It looked like playing. I don't know of any study on the phenomenon of play in birds.

"Gwen!"

I have to make an effort to stay with the piece we're playing. I keep thinking about the Crow, about the tops of the pine trees.

"That's better. Next, Elgar's 'Enigma Variations'. Just the strings this afternoon. The rest of you can go home. Now, a ten-minute break. And it's 'Nimrod', for those who wish to get themselves ready."

He comes and stands beside me. "I do understand that you're going through a lot at the moment. Your father's death, your family's reaction."

"Swifts."

"Pardon?" He twirls his moustache, keeping his eyes fixed on the door.

"That piece by Elgar, it makes me think of Swifts. They only settle on the earth to breed. They sleep in the air, eat in the air."

He walks off in the rhythm we were just playing, slowing himself down at the door, so that he finishes at exactly the right point.

Joan comes and sits beside me. A Seagull flies past again. I hardly ever see them here. Perhaps they can't find enough to eat by the coast. "Do you think my tempo isn't right? In my opinion, it's his tempo that's wrong."

I turn towards her. "Perhaps you should discuss that with Stockdale, not me."

"He blows his top so fast." That tic again.

I try not to sound irritated. "It's always like that. He gets cross, you lose confidence, and then it goes from bad to worse."

"But do you think I'm playing it right or not?"

I shrug my shoulders. "I think the truth lies somewhere in between."

Priscilla joins us. "Do you think the weather will hold? Ken and I want to go sailing this weekend."

Joan thinks it will get colder. I move to the window—always the same kind of chitchat. Priscilla is really nice, with her rosy cheeks—apple cheeks, as Olive would say—and her flaxen hair, and she's amusing, and I like Joan too, so I don't know why I'm feeling so annoyed. Two bobbies are walking past outside. I tap my fingers restlessly against my leg: 'Nimrod'.

I don't want to go straight home after the rehearsal. The city is too loud today. Late spring is heavy in the elm trees in Battersea Park: song, blossom, chubby little Blackbirds and Sparrows, an empty eggshell here and there. Young people walk past me—laughing, flirting, quarrelling—this is the best season for dreaming. Soon it will be too hot and the thick, grimy air will thrust us further out of the city. An older couple are sitting on a bench, coats closed, in spite of the heat. She takes his hand.

There's a group of students walking in the gardens. They stop by the Memorial sculpture, some of them sketching the figures in their books. Thomas also loves this monument. I carry on, past the bees in the Old English Garden, past the lake, till I reach the old oak tree where the Great Tits are nesting. There is a little bench opposite, far enough from the nest not to disturb them. It is a while before the parents arrive—I can't see the nest itself, it's near the top of the tree, in a little hollow. I take my notebook out of my violin case. I'm writing an article about the song of Great Tits. I've read a number of studies on birdsong over the past few years. Its structure has been intensively researched, but very little has been written about its meaning. So whenever I have a few hours to spare I go to this place in the park, and note down the songs and calls of a particular group of birds, at the same time recording their relationships and interactions. By the end of the spring I hope I'll have gathered enough information to make a really good piece of work.

One of the young Great Tits flies out of a lavender bush a little further on, lands right by my feet and hops towards me. "Hallo, little one," I say to him. He tilts his head, takes another step forward, but then swiftly flies away again.

*   *   *

"Lennie?" Thomas is lying on his back, smoking.

"Hmm." A boat sails past. I can see the old man at the tiller very clearly. He can't see us.

"Would you like to marry me?"

I move from the window to the bed. Wind shifts the water, the swell making the boat bob. I sit down beside him and place my hand on his wrist. "No."

"Are you sure?" He sits up. "I could buy a house, a real house. We'd be happy."

"Have you been talking to your mother?" I close my hand around his wrist, open it again.

"That's not the reason. We've been together so long."

I raise an eyebrow.

"We've known each other so long now." He takes my hand. "I love you."

"Well, I love you too. I just don't want to get married. And certainly not to you." I caress his red curls.

"You're insufferable."

"You too. Why do you want this again, all of a sudden?"

He sighs. "She wants me to get married, to start a family. Otherwise…"

"Otherwise you can whistle for your money." My tone isn't indignant—I knew it. He remains silent.

"I'm not going to play along. Sorry. If you really want to get married, do so, but ask one of your other girlfriends."

"But you're the only one. The only one I love. We've known each other so long now." A pleading look from someone who really is too old to play the little boy any more.

"Seriously, Thomas. You know just as well as I do that we should never live in a house together."

"Do you have a better idea?"

I've told him about the legacy. "Has she given you an ultimatum?" I ask.

"A year, and then she'll stop my allowance."

I laugh. "You'll have to pull out all the stops, old chap."
He lets go of my hand, turns away from me. "I'm sorry."

"No, I should have been much clearer from the start. That
you were the one, not the others."

He's trying hard, harder than last time. I take a cigarette
too, light it, and inhale deeply. He'll look for someone else,
a pretty girl, young, pliable. He'll marry her, have children,
and will keep seeing me till it's no longer possible, or until
I no longer wish it.

We smoke in silence. In silence I get dressed.

He follows me to the door.

"Did you really think I'd say yes?"

"I don't know." The answer that people give when they
don't want to say something else. He opens the door for me.
In his eyes I see the reflection of the road behind me.

On the path along the Thames women are strolling in short-
sleeved frocks, men without their overcoats. It's going to be
another hot day. Flowers bow to the sun. In the spinney in
front of the station boys in short trousers are playing with
little stones, knees brown with dirt, sand on their hands.
Children. Scenery. I'm walking here and could just as well
be walking somewhere else. People look at me, then forget
they've ever seen me.

There's a throng of people at the station entrance—is
it eight o'clock? Nine o'clock? The day has begun. It has
long been light. I could take a train—I have enough money
now—go to a hotel on the coast, for just a night, or two, the
violin in its case by the door.

On Friday I'm playing in a premiere. I still have to practise.
I quicken my pace. Someone is singing in one of the houses.
A bus drives past, but I overtake it when it halts at a bus stop.
The water in the river beside me is flowing back to the boat.
The plane trees by the path were here when we first walked
this way. All those footsteps sealed in the asphalt. The park,
the cemetery—and it's only when I reach the school again
that I hear people, not just the cooing of Pigeons.

I knock at the door. Jenny opens, morning miss, a little nod,
a curtsey. I go up the stairs two steps at a time. The Great Tit
he sketched for me, on a brown paper bag, still hangs by the
window. I take up my violin and play to the Great Tit. The
music streams through the open window, is drowned by the
sounds of the city.

*   *   *

Dodie opens the door. I crouch down in front of her. "Hallo,
cheeky. Is your Mummy at home?" She says nothing in reply,
but fixes her eyes on me, her pale little face looking very
serious.

Thea calls out from the back room. "Len? Come in. I'm
feeding Lila." Joey comes to take a look at me too. I squeeze
past them through the passage, bending my head to avoid
the washing.

"I'm sorry it's such a mess. We just don't have enough
space." She gives me a broad grin as I enter. "Well, what do
you know, she's dropped off now."

I stroke Lila's cheek. She's a person already, although
not fully.

"If you want something to drink, you'll have to see to it yourself."

"Later. Do you want something?"

She shakes her head, gently rocking Lila back and forth.

"When is Don back?" Don is a soloist now, with the London Symphony Orchestra, in which Thea also used to play. They're touring Europe.

"Tonight." She tells me about Lila, who already sleeps the whole night through sometimes. The children's voices mingle with hers, with the deep, distant drone of machines in the factory on the other side of the street. The city seems to be growing louder and louder.

"Thomas wants to marry me."

"Again?" Thea gives a little shake of her head as she looks at me.

"I believe he really means it."

"I'm sure he does." She sighs.

"But he isn't faithful. He isn't the marrying kind. Me neither."

"You could do it. And then just carry on as you are." Her face expresses optimism, her voice sounds dubious.

"I walked home by the river yesterday, and saw how it would be. I could go back. He was busy painting the Thames again, the view from his boat, his fourth one."

"Mine!" Dodie runs into the room with Joey close behind. He's trying to snatch a wooden train from her hand—and when that doesn't work, he tugs at her pinafore, and then Dodie screams. Thea intervenes, puts Dodie in a corner with her train and gives Joey a crust of bread.

"How are things in the orchestra now?"

"Same as ever. We're playing Tchaikovsky."

"So you're in that phase again. What about your research?"

"I'm reading a book at the moment about how they condition Pigeons. Really nasty work." I tell her about the way the Pigeons are trained, with food and electric shocks. "You know what I think: that it's not only immoral to study birds in lab conditions, but it's also bad science. They behave differently then. The birds we had at home when I was young were much cleverer than this kind of research suggests."

"Joey, leave your sister alone!"

I stand up. "Would you like a cup of tea?" When I'm in the kitchen I put the kettle on and make a start on the washing up. Just enough light falls through the octagonal windowpanes onto the work surface.

"Len, don't wash up," Thea calls from the sitting room. I pretend not to hear.

When I go back to the room, everything is peaceful. Joey is playing in a corner with the train. Dodie is dressing a doll. Thea puts Lila into her cradle. I give her a cup of tea, luke-warm, milky and sugary, just as she likes it.

"You didn't wash up, did you, Len?"

"Is this how you thought it would be?" I tilt my head to catch her eye.

She laughs. "No. And it's not what I wanted either. But it's fine. When Don's home again, I'll have some breathing space."

"Don't you miss performing?"

She shakes her head. "No time for that." Lila starts to cry. "Would you like to hold her a while?" Thea rocks her back and forth, till she has calmed down, and then puts her in my arms. "That suits you. But listen, I've got something to tell you. We're probably going to emigrate, to Canada. Don wants to go back. He can get a position there too."

"Really? And you think it would work out?"

"It's so beautiful there." She has a dreamy look. "Wilderness. Untouched forests, wild creatures. And it always snows in the winter."

I don't tell her she could go to Scotland for that. Lila gazes at me and I sing softly to her, about a fat little mouse that has left its nest for the very first time, until she falls asleep, and wakes up again two seconds later and starts crying.

*   *   *

"Billie!" Stockdale silences the orchestra with a swift movement of the hand. The premiere is tomorrow and he's not at all happy.

"Come on," I say. "Just let us play right through, for once. You yourself don't know exactly what you want. One moment it's Joan's fault, then Billie's, and then someone else's, but you're not setting the right tempo."

Everyone looks at me in amazement. It's an unwritten rule that we simply accept Stockdale's fits of temper. He's the boss. There's a story about a clarinettist, Sasha, who answered him back once. She was never hired anywhere again. It was before my time and the story has, of course, been embroidered.

The silence grows deeper, until someone finally coughs— Priscilla, or one of the other cellists.

"So. And you know better, do you? Perhaps you'd like to stand here then. Put your violin down."

"I don't know better. It's just that it's always the same." I speak loudly and clearly. "You start a little too slow, for the upbeat and the first few bars, and then you begin to speed up and that's the point where it all goes wrong. So, either you should start at a swifter tempo, or you should stick with us after the first bar."

"Come on then." He is slowly turning red. His fingers are white around his baton.

"I don't want to quarrel with you. But I'm not the only one who thinks this."

"Oh, is that right? Not the only one." He taps his baton on the palm of his other hand, controlled, deliberate and in the correct time.

I glance behind me—no one is backing me up, no one makes eye contact, everyone is waiting till this is over. Fine. Let them sort it out themselves. "Well then. Are we going to continue?"

Stockdale gives the upbeat, quicker than before. We play the whole piece just a little too swiftly, but all the way through to the end, and a little too loudly; the nerves need to be expressed, apparently.

"Gwen," Stockdale says as I'm putting my violin in its case. "Do you have a moment?"

Joan walks past, her face averted. So, no support from her either.

"I'm sorry I said it in front of the others." I look directly at him. The colour of his face has returned to normal.

"So they talk about it, do they?"

"Everyone talks about everything and sometimes about you."

He briefly clenches his fists. "The gossip here is unhealthy!"

"Is that all you have to say?"

"Come on, Gwen. Seen like that, it's all a case of much ado about nothing. We're off to the bar. And practise with that baton a little, since you're such an expert."

*　　　*　　　*

On Sunday I walk back by the same route, along the Thames, which lays its waves over noise, absorbing sounds, returning them, not as echoes but as wind. I was walking swiftly when I set off, but at the station I'm passed by city gents, at the water by day trippers, where the path narrows by children with buckets and spades on their way to the riverbank, and where the ash trees start I can't go on. I sit down on a tree stump. Three steps further and I would be able to see the boat.

A Magpie lands in front of me, snatches something from the ground, and flies up. A few weeks ago I wrote a response to a study on the language of Magpies—they'd been totally isolated from their kind and treated like machines, and that was the inevitable result of the experiment too; and yet Magpies are really sociable birds, who can be taught anything. My letter was published. The editor wrote back to me and asked if I also did scientific research.

An older man, with a walking stick, tips his hat to me in greeting. I've seen him here before—he lives somewhere in the area. I wave back.

Two Crows land not far from my feet. They have something to discuss. They don't hold it back.

I stand up, pat the dirt off my skirt, breathe in. A woman's voice is calling something, laughing. She is blonde, young, taller than me and slender. Thomas is holding her arm, and he's laughing too, his face alight. He only sees me when I'm really close.

"Len. I thought…" He shakes his head. "I thought that you, that we…"

The young woman looks at him. "Is there a problem? Should I leave?"

He looks at me.

"No," I say. "It's nothing."

He stays silent as I walk away, and is still silent when I reach the end of the sandy path and turn around to look at him—she's talking, she raises her hand. The distance. I nod, to myself or to the people walking towards me, and follow the path up the bank.

At home I pick up my violin in the hope that playing it will make me feel better. I tune it, play a couple of scales. But I remain a woman in a room with a piece of wood in her hands. This has happened before and the only thing to do is to keep on playing, so that's what I do. But the aversion stays, growing out in different directions, like a tree, twigs protruding from my ears and mouth.

I walk to my desk and pick up my notes. The Great Tits have various alarm calls, and I have now identified three—one for people, one for large birds in the sky, and one for creatures down below. There will certainly be more, but the problem is that there is an enormous individual variation in their calls. Moreover, the notes follow each other so swiftly that I always have the feeling that I, with my human ears, have missed something. I should try to become more proficient at this, but I don't know how I could combine that with playing the violin.

Jenny rings the bell from the bottom of the stairs. It's time for tea again. I close my notebook. If I don't leave, then this is all I can expect.

*   *   *

Thea's uncle owns a holiday cabin near Brighton, where I can stay for a few weeks at very little cost. I can work on my article in peace there. Stockdale thought it was a good idea, and I no longer have any worries about money. Mr Williams said it was real countryside there. The hut is located by a heath, near the Downs and close to the sea. The nearest railway station is half an hour's walk away.

I've seen nothing of Thomas since that encounter by the Thames. But there have been other times in the past when we haven't been in touch. And now, after all, I do want to let him know where I'm going, before I leave. And I want to know how things stand.

The fog makes me unsure of the route. It's the third day now that it has shrouded the city, and although things haven't vanished they're mostly invisible. I turn left too soon, retrace my steps. It's the next street, and I don't understand how I could have gone wrong. The Thames doesn't think, it just keeps on flowing—I can only see the water's edge, grey and still, but soft white below, a cloud bed.

The gravel on the path is damp, slippery; I take care on the gangplank. I knock twice.

"Len. Good to see you." Thomas's voice is still sleepy. "Like some coffee?"

"Yes please. I won't stay long."

There's a pile of dirty plates in the kitchen. I sit down at the low wooden table. "I'm going away for a while."

"Marvellous. Where are you off to?"

I feel it, when he looks at me. I swallow. "Nowhere special, just away."

"Yes, you deserve that occasionally. You always work so hard. Do you know when you'll be back?" He puts the coffee in front of me.

I shake my head.

"Shall I show you my new series?"

I follow him to the front of the boat. In the first painting two Crows are flying above the houses of London. "They're dancing," I say. Every colour can be seen in the black of their feathers.

He gives an enthusiastic nod. "And this one." A young Crow is sitting on the lowest branch of an elm tree, watching the ground intently, ready to hunt. His concentration is tangible. And there are more: an old Crow with her eyes tightly shut in the rain; a flock of Crows mobbing an intruder.

"They're wonderful." Two Crows on a nest, both of them looking at something in the distance.

"Stay."

I turn towards him. "I don't want it any more. It's so loud here, so filthy. Mrs Willows from across the road died last week, of pneumonia. And the orchestra stifles me—always the same old gossip, who's having an affair with whom, all that hullabaloo with Stockdale."

"Len, you must play. Find a new orchestra."

"I want to study birds. Seriously, I mean."

"I don't think there's any call for that kind of thing. Not that I don't find it interesting. I just mean, the times aren't ripe for it yet. And you haven't any education in that field." He falls silent when he sees the look I give him, and takes my arm. I don't yield. He moves towards me. I move back.

"Sorry, I don't want coffee after all. I just wanted to say hallo."

He looks at me, keeps looking while I put on my coat, open the door, vanish into the grey.

STAR 8

At the end of February it became clear that Baldhead was far too weak to raise a new brood. He would come to me for nuts, then close his eyes and nestle on my lap until I stood up again. For days Star tried to encourage Baldhead to help her build a nest, swooping down in exactly the same way that she had seen him doing the previous year—Great Tits often imitate the behaviour of others to encourage them to do something. It was no use, and Star transferred her attentions to Peetur. For a few days she flew back and forth between Baldhead and Peetur, until one day Baldhead made a little rush at her. Then Star decided to choose Peetur instead and Baldhead found a new roosting place, in a nest box on the other side of the garden.

Just as Baldhead had done, Peetur also wanted to sleep in the nest box with Star. Once again Star opposed this. However, Peetur was a more creative singer than Baldhead, and each time he used different notes to express his displeasure. On the first night he was driven away for hours before Star finally let him in; his vocabulary was certainly more extensive at the end of that day! It seemed that Star enjoyed listening to his newly discovered language; when he sang she would often pop her head out to look at him. Peetur also seemed to derive much pleasure from singing: after that first evening he knew that she would eventually give in.

Baldhead stayed in the house a great deal. In March he still had a good appetite, and Monocle enticed him into making a nest with her. He did make a half-hearted attempt to furnish the nest, but he no longer had the strength to defend it and to bring up the nestlings. So Monocle had to care for her brood alone, although now and again he would take a look at them. *The swelling above his bill, which he had suffered from years before, had now returned, and he often had a listless look in his eyes. I knew he would not live long now.*

As always, Star took great pains in building her nest. She had discovered that the threads from the Persian rug in the sitting room were perfect for this, and she flew back and forth with beakfuls. I rolled up the rug and put it in the passage, but she swiftly realised what I had done, so I put the rug back; it was better for her to pluck from the whole carpet than to make bald patches at its edges.

At the beginning of April Star tried to chase another pair of Great Tits, Dusty and Cross, away from her part of the garden. Dusty and Cross were an older pair; they had built a nest near the path the previous year, but that had now been taken by others. There was enough room in the garden and I did not understand why Star wanted to expel them. She was extremely determined, but so was Dusty, and when she drove Dusty off even after she had laid her eggs, I decided to intervene—Dusty had as much right to the garden as Star. I kept chasing Star away if she came anywhere near Dusty's nest. Star could not be stopped; she avoided me but was twice as fierce with Dusty when I was not around. She succeeded so well in making Dusty lose heart that she deserted her nest and found a new place in the neighbouring garden. It was really strange to see Star act so obsessively; in the past she was well able to share space with others.

At the end of May her eggs hatched and then I understood why she had driven Dusty off: it had been a long, wet winter and there was insufficient food for two nests. I felt ashamed, and finally realised that Great Tits have a better understanding of what is good for them than I do.

1937

I brush the dust off the table and unpack my suitcase. What would Billie and Joan and Thea think if they could see me now, in this wooden hut with only a bed, a camp stove and a cupboard for my towels and clothing? And then I take off my suit, put my bathing costume on, dark blue to light blue, and walk down the narrow path through the back garden to the river. Poppies, cornflowers, buttercups. The water is clear and cool. I walk straight into the middle of the river, then sink into the water. For a moment I gasp for breath, and then swim, my hair waterweed, my hands water brown. I duck down and touch the bottom; the soft sand makes opaque smudges in the water. I rise to the surface, float on my back. The sun draws patterns on my eyelids, honeycomb cells. I shut them tight—the shapes shrink and grow, change to little circles and specks that swim away. A noise makes me jump. I open my eyes, twist my body round: a Duck. She accepts my presence as completely natural, although people seldom come here. Perhaps that's exactly why. I cough and it startles her. "Sorry!"

By a willow tree I turn back. I swim homewards, with slow strokes. Time here is hardly more than a change of the light.

I lay two towels on the bed and lie down on my back. The rhythm of the train is still in my body; my mind is full of voices, the people in the London station, in the packed train carriage—human beings are hardly aware of how much they talk, how loud they are. Only yesterday evening I gave a performance for the mayor; this morning I said farewell to the children. Dear God! Poor little Bertie, with his dandruff and filthy face. Eleven years old, and his life is already mapped out: factory, wife, children—eight, nine, ten of them. Leah, Janet, Josie, working in the laundry already, a couple of days a week. These children won't have anyone to teach them music now. Billie is supposed to be taking over, but she won't have time till September. I cough again. Perhaps I'm getting a cold—but it's hot, about eighty-six degrees, and the water evaporating from my body cools me down. I mustn't imagine that I'm so important to them. I can only give them music, one short hour each week.

I sit up. There's a huge spider's web behind the bed. The summer has just started and there are so many spiders already. I have no idea what this indicates. That cough again. I should take a drink of water. I wade through the heat to the little kitchen. A plate. No glass. I drink from the tap.

I open my violin case, and tune up on the bed. My playing disturbs the silence, makes me too large, too present, too melancholic. I put the violin back. Another time, perhaps.

The late light that seems so much clearer here, because we're close to the sea, slowly lets itself be driven away. When darkness finally falls, the Blackbirds are still singing. My neighbours. Too tired for sleep, I stay on the veranda. The willows are absorbed into the darkness, and then come back, one by one. Sentinels.

*　　　*　　　*

"Billie!"

"Gwen!" She takes hold of me and kisses my cheek. "But what's this? You did write in your letter that it was a real hut, but not that it was so primitive! How can you bear it?"

"I can practise here, and swim, and the air's clean." The heat has lodged in my body, made me slow, languid and passive.

"But it's the back of beyond here. I had to walk for half an hour and I only met a few cows on the way. Is it such a trek when you go shopping too?" She gives an exaggerated sigh, mops her forehead, wipes her hand on her culottes.

"Mr Williams has lent me his pushbike."

She shakes her head. "Well, it certainly suits you, this seclusion."

"Shall we go for a swim? You brought your bathing costume, did you? Or we could go for a walk, perhaps. Just a little distance, and then you're on the Downs. I saw Chiffchaffs up there yesterday, Blackcaps, Redstarts, Goldfinches."

She sits down and pulls off her shoes. "I've walked quite enough already, thanks. But what about a little drink?" She kneads her hair with her hands.

"It's one o'clock!"

"I'm on holiday!" She stretches her legs out towards the door.

"I'll make a cup of tea first."

From the kitchen I ask her how things are with the orchestra, with her fiancé. I look out of the window at the garden, at the rolling landscape beyond.

The Blackbird, whom I've called Ollie because he reminds me of my sister, is perched on the windowsill. I set a raisin down for him. Billie comes and stands in the doorway and grimaces. "Ugh, what *are* you doing?"

"They're really tame round here. And we always had birds in and around our house, in the past." Ollie takes the raisin and swoops off with it to the willow, flying swiftly through the drooping branches.

"But don't they cause diseases? All those bacteria. And lice. I read recently that all birds have lice. And mites too. Disgusting. Oh, hang on, I've got something for you."

She takes a package out of her bag; it contains a women's magazine, a bar of chocolate, a bottle of Madeira and a pair of stockings. "From Joan and me."

I thank her, then leaf through the magazine.

"Oh, cripes!" She stands up, takes a step back, rigid, her body bent slightly backwards, the corners of her mouth turned down.

A spider is sauntering across the edge of the table. I let him walk onto my hand, then from my hand onto the grass outside.

Billie sits down again, more straight-backed than necessary.

"Do you think things are improving? Do you feel less stifled now? Does the fresh air help?"

"A bit." It's not the air, but the space; not the space, but time; not time, but the light.

Billie tells me that Stockdale now goes everywhere with Deborah, the new violin player.

"Typical! Shall we go for a swim soon?"

"And I think Joan has got something going on with Barry."

"Who's Barry?"

"Barry Heaton. You know. The trumpet player."

I do vaguely remember him, the timbre of his voice, not his face; he played in the orchestra a while, when I was new there. A good player, someone you don't really notice because he does exactly what he should.

"Do you hear that?" I point outside.

She shakes her head.

"That Great Tit. He comes here a lot. I recognise him by that little motif." I imitate it. "It's more complex than it seems, with all those semitones and then the trill at the end."

She frowns, nods.

"Their song is different here. Not like it is in London." I get hold of my notebook, let her see the fragments of bird-song I've notated.

"So?"

"No one knows exactly what they're saying. There've been a lot of studies of birdsong, but mainly on its structure, not its meaning."

"I always assumed they sang to win a female and protect their territory. Like most men." She laughs.

"I think they're saying much more than that."

Billie picks up the bottle of Madeira. "Holidays!"

I bring the table outside and while she tells me about her fiancé, I watch the flowers gently swaying. The space between us doubles and doubles, until Billie is miles away. A Goose honks in the distance.

*   *   *

In the morning I follow the course of the little brook that flows southwards, past the hut. It leads to a pond, cut off from the sea by a dyke studded with seashells. Its water takes on the colour of the sky, mirrors the day. Last week there were farm horses here, thick tufts of hair on their fetlocks. Freed from their harness, they raced around and rolled onto their backs, until the first horse trotted into the pond. The second horse watched him, then also trotted in. The rest followed, like foals. When I see them now, pulling the plough, so quietly and strongly, I think about their secret life, the joy behind their serious bearing.

I sit at the edge of the water, in grass so light in colour that it seems grey. Ringed Plovers skitter across the sand on the other side. Just a fortnight more, and then I have to return to London. I don't even know now where I put my violin. Something is moving in the bush beside me. I keep as still as possible. A hazel dormouse, or some other kind of dormouse, off and away before I can properly see him. A bumble bee lands on my calf, its fat little feet tickling me.

Countless small birds emerge from the scrub, first the Sparrows, then the Goldfinches, a Redbreast, a Wagtail, a Wren—they're taking a look at me, like villagers who come out to greet a newly arrived guest, and then they carry on with whatever was keeping them busy. This shining land is not ours. Because I keep completely still, the birds behave exactly as they would otherwise do. I've learned more about their behaviour in ten days here than during all those years in London. Because people are so full of their own importance, they don't see other creatures correctly—yet simply to describe their behaviour with precision would place everything in a different light.

A Woodcock lands in the grass. Clouds shift white across the water. My reluctance increases with every step down the dyke.

*   *   *

The staircase is full of smoke. I let my feet feel their way down the narrow stairs, skid a little, try not to breathe, it's a question of seconds, not minutes, the last steps, the front door, no key, I pound and pound and call out, cough, someone's screaming on the other side of the door, pounding, screaming. I take shallow breaths, in, out, in, out, can't breathe any more.

Wood, a slam, a man's voice, an opening. Air.

I don't know if I was making some kind of sound, but the woman opposite me—dark-blue stockings, a little cloche hat in the same colour—glances up from her book and gives me a disapproving look. I'm not as well groomed as I was on the outward journey. And much less concerned about it. I give her a smile. She purses her lips and pretends to carry on with her book. Her husband is looking at the landscape. His white moustache bobs to the rhythm of the train. He's humming.

I take my little black notebook out of my bag, yawning. The ceremony is at ten o'clock, and it will take me at least an hour to get to the church. To try and shake off my sleepiness, I make sketches of the woman and the man. When we reach Blackfriars, I put the notebook away.

The city greets me with rain. And after three streets I know that I'm wearing the wrong shoes. I stop walking at the first bus stop I can find. My umbrella knocks against someone else's, a man in a hurry. The streets are shining, showing an upside-down city that is constantly broken by traffic. Machines rumble in the distance, a military band that never comes closer. For the whole bus journey, jammed between damp coats and voices and hair, I play a violin part in my head to drown out the sound. It smells of people, of human bodies.

Joan is standing on the pavement outside the church. She's smoking and only spots me when I get closer. She embraces me, holding the arm with the cigarette behind her. "Gwennie. So good to see you." Her eyes look sad.

"Isn't Barry here?"

She shakes her head, takes a last puff from the cigarette. "He's on reconnaissance, in France. They're expecting all sorts to happen. I'll go in with you." She stubs the cigarette out, links arms with me; for a moment we truly are friends.

The steps are made of marble and are slippery with rain. Joan loses her footing, but my arm steadies her, prevents a fall. She smiles at the door as if nothing has happened.

"How are things in the hut? Doesn't the silence send you crazy? It would drive me up the wall. Billie said she wouldn't be able to stand it."

"I like peace and quiet." The stone floor of the church has been worn smooth by thousands, tens of thousands of feet, past and present together, silently supporting all those years.

"Me too, but not isolation." She looks at herself in her compact mirror, combs her grey hair into shape with her hand.

Stockdale enters, arm in arm with a long-legged girl—a young deer, a hind, that must be Deborah. He waves, but shows no intention of approaching me. Behind him is Joey, the double bass player, as rosy-cheeked as ever; Emile, the bassoonist, is talking to him, his voice over-reedy for his body. People greet each other, always looking across each other's shoulders to check if another acquaintance is arriving, someone more important.

We sit down in the third row, by the aisle. I greet people on all sides, take off my shoes to massage my feet, under the bench, under the old wood, the rack for the prayer books. I prod through my stocking, making a hole in the blister. It stings. Joan is chatting to the man beside her, one of Billie's uncles.

I cough. My fingertips are tingling. At first I try not to notice my breathing, and then do precisely that. The church organ starts playing. People continue to talk for a few moments, and then fall silent and turn around. Billie is led forward by her father. She's wearing a white dress, simple and elegant, trimmed with lace, and a white cap with a veil. I think of the water, the rain on the roof of the hut, about my article, and about Ollie the Blackbird, who came indoors this morning and perched on the table.

*   *   *

I can only breathe normally again when I'm in the train. I now understand why my father wanted to live in Wales, although he wasn't at all suited to country life. It's quiet in the compartment. I take off my shoes, take out my notebook to write. The sun outside is a red ball.

"Len?"

A dart hurtles from my eyes to my mouth to my heart, my diaphragm, my abdomen. "Thomas."

He leans down, gives me a kiss on the cheek, sits opposite me. "Crikey, what a coincidence. I was thinking of you today. Where are you off to?"

"To Sussex." I tell him about the hut, calling it a holiday cottage, and describe the river and the Ducks, the Blackbird in the kitchen, the grass, the light, the long days.

I don't mention the old desire, which awakens in spite of me.

"So you really did leave." His curls are a little longer than they were; he is less thin. "Can you manage without performing though? How do you get through the day?"

"How's Donna?" I don't look at him as I ask the question. I found out accidentally, from a newspaper announcement.

"Oh, Donna. Yes. Very well. Expecting. Who'd have thought it, hey? Have you seen this sky?" He moves his face into my field of view, catches my eye with his own. "And how are you?"

"None of your business." I gaze out of the window, at the world waiting there.

"Too late. The story of my life."

I look at him. "Oh, don't moan. Your wife's expecting a baby." Half angry, half mocking.

He laughs. "You're absolutely right. I'm sorry. Still. Marriage. Perhaps you were right. Perhaps you are right."

"I went to Billie's wedding."

"She married the Yank, right? How did it go?"

"As it should. In a church, everyone dressed to the nines. Joan had a good weep. Stockdale was there with his new lady friend. But it mainly felt strange and distant." We've passed Haywards Heath now—buildings have switched to trees.

"These things always do."

"Are you happy?" Words like clumsy boats, running aground long before they reach the shore.

"Contented." He doesn't look at me.

We talk until he gets out at Burgess Hill to visit a friend. I see him enter the small white wooden station building. Not so long ago this would have opened it all up again. Now the train simply moves on, past fawn-coloured cattle and fields full of sheep, hedges, bare twisted trees, Wivelsfield, a pond. The red in the sky has turned lilac, then purple, then dark blue, the shadow of the earth silhouetted against the pink, and now it's become a blanket full of stars, little openings that let the light shine through.

*   *   *

I tune my violin. We're playing Rachmaninoff's Second Symphony. Stockdale has made a revised version, to cut down on its length. I wipe rosin onto the bow. They were delighted to see me, as if I'd been away three months instead of three weeks. As if I'm the same person I was three weeks ago. "Maestro?"

He looks up at me, annoyed, holding his finger in the score.

"Could I have a word with you?"

"Can we do that later? When we're finished?"

He doesn't see my nod. He's turned his head already.

Priscilla opens the window. The way she moves it's as if she's a much older woman. The odour of the green room mingles with the scents of late summer, the grating strings with distant voices and the noise of the city. I yawn, go in search of a coffee. From the passageway I can see into the foyer: ladies in evening gowns, men in dress suits, barmaids, smoke. I feel nothing at all—no enthusiasm, not even that nervous tension bordering on fear.

I play as well as ever. It feels like a betrayal.

I leave the building with Stockdale. "I want to stop." Ashtree leaves spin around on the street in a little whirlwind.

"Yes, you've said something like that already. You can't have it both ways. But you will finish this season, won't you?"

I glance sideways, can only see irritation in his face, not our shared history.

"If you wish."

"I wish nothing. You signed a contract." He quickens his pace, lets two other people come between us, before he catches up with Deborah. I don't know what I expected.

I run a few steps, till I'm beside him again. "But the contract only finishes next year."

"Then we'll have plenty of time to find a good substitute."

"I want to leave earlier than that."

He asks Deborah if she'd like to go to the bar.

"Harold, I'm extremely grateful to you for everything. But it's enough now. You have nothing to gain if I no longer play well."

"We'll discuss it some other time." He takes Deborah's arm and coaxes her across the street. Joan comes and walks with me. "What was all that about?"

"I want to give it up."

She's clearly taken aback. "Completely?"

We cross the road, nipping swiftly past a bus that stirs the air behind my back. More body, less spirit, that's what I'm becoming.

Joan keeps questioning me, clearly happy about the space I'll leave when I'm gone: less competition—I'm one of the oldest members, one of the best players.

The wind ruffles coats, freshens my face. I tell her I intend to study birds, explain how I'd set up my research.

"Right," she says, and frowns a little, then laughs to let me know she means well.

During the night the wind dies down, as if something has yielded, something that the world accepted far sooner than me.

STAR 9

At the end of June I tried to tempt Star back. All the youngsters had flown the nest and summer had really begun. The birds once more had time for other activities. Star ignored me and did not wish to accept any peanuts. I had clearly insulted her by chasing her off when she was treating Dusty so unkindly. Not until August did she become more approachable, and when she had come for a nut a few times, I again attempted to interest her in counting. One morning I tapped three times on the screen near the window. It gave her a shock, because I had used the same noise to drive her away from Dusty. She immediately flew off, scolding me loudly. I decided not to tap any more and enticed her purely with peanuts, which after a little while she accepted again from me. My friendship with her was more important than the experiment, and perhaps we could begin afresh the following year.

One chilly morning in September she tapped, of her own accord, four times on the window frame, and then I rewarded her with a nut. But afterwards, when I tried to give her a number, she gave no reaction. The next morning I tapped five times for her. She swooped towards me, threatening, then scolded me from the window ledge for a long time.

1938

"Bird Cottage," I say to Theo McIver. "That's what I'll call it."

"There are certainly plenty of birds," he says. We're in the sitting room, which is neither too big nor too small—there's enough space for a table and four chairs, a sofa in front of the fireplace, and a piano. The bookcases can be put against the wall on the kitchen side. Theo has just shown me the bedroom, which looks out onto the orchard. The bathroom has to be retiled, but the bath—with its claw feet—is in good condition. There is a little terrace in front of the kitchen. The garden that surrounds the house is sufficiently large. The hedge has to be trimmed, the grass must be mown, the trees are all in good condition. There is enough space for a vegetable garden, although I don't know if that's a good idea with the birds. "My old man let things get a little run-down over the past twenty years, but that's reflected in the price. It'll cost you something to have renovated, but it'll still come out cheap." He draws his hand through his blond curls and grins.

"Neighbours?"

"Doris lives over there. She's an old widow." He points to the small dwelling to the left of the house. "On the other side of the lane are the Hendersons, in that little house in front of the woods. Fine people. And far enough away not to bother you. This used to be a farm; the land went all the way to that hedge over there, but my father sold that plot after my mother's death."

There are dark, heavy clouds above the Downs. "Would you live here?"

"No, I like living close to other people."

"The village is ten minutes' walk away."

"Exactly." He gives me a triumphant look.

"Well, you'll never sell a house like that."

He laughs. "This house doesn't need my help to sell it. Everyone's keen to live here and the price of land goes up each year. There was a man here yesterday, looking for a holiday cottage. He's a serious buyer, but I'd rather sell it to someone who'll make it their home."

We walk back with each other along Lewes Road to South Street. Just before we reach the crossroads where he has his grocer's shop, it begins to pour. He opens the door, the bell tinkles. "Would you like a cuppa?"

"Yes please." I wipe the drops of rain from my forehead and follow him through the little shop to the space behind the counter.

"Mary, this is Gwendolen. She's interested in Dad's house. Gwendolen, this is Mary, my wife."

A young woman, with exactly the same kind of curls as Theo, gives my hand a gentle shake. "Awful weather, isn't it? I was hoping you'd make it back in time." She stands up and I see her belly.

"Your first?"

Theo gives a proud nod. "Wonderful, eh? You're not married?" He gives me a curious look, then is shocked at his own question. "Sorry. It's none of my business."

"You're allowed to ask. The right moment didn't come along. Things turned out differently."

"You're still young."

I brush the comment aside with a wave of my hand. We both know I'm no longer young.

Mary places a strong cup of tea in front of me and a small jug of milk. She turns the radio down.

I take a lump of sugar from the bowl. "Are things going well with your business?"

"So-so. People are short of money, because of the slump. That's why we need to sell the house quickly." He asks if I can tell him my decision this week, so that he'll know if he has to opt for the other buyer. I promise to contact him swiftly. They wave goodbye to me, hand in hand, like children.

The next morning I go to the bank. I wait behind a man in dirty trousers. He pours coins onto the counter out of a paper bag and speaks in a dialect I don't recognise. He winks at me as he leaves.

"How may I help you?" The man behind the counter has a beaky nose and greasy hair.

"I'd like to withdraw the money from my savings account." I place the savings book on the counter.

He picks it up, gives it a brief glance, then lays it down again. "I will need Mr Howard's signature."

"There is no Mr Howard." I smile.

He turns the book towards me. "The account was opened by Newman Howard. So I need his signature."

"My father passed away last year."

"You will have to prove that. You need to ask for a death certificate, fill in these forms, and then return them to us. The process will take about six weeks."

"I don't have that much time." I tap my fingers on the counter.

He shrugs.

"Please." The man doesn't answer. I clench my fists, release them. "May I speak to the manager?"

"He is not available."

"Then I'll wait." I sit down on a hard wooden chair by the window. The man walks away, then returns and serves the old man who was in the queue behind me.

I think about the house, which is exactly right, and then about my father.

After half an hour a small man fetches me. He takes me to his office, which is blue with smoke. The desk is piled high with papers. I explain the problem.

"Why do you wish to buy this house so much?" He lights a cigar.

I tell him that I plan to study birds. "The house is perfect for that. I already saw so many birds there. It's an excellent location. I could start my research immediately."

"I was a keen bird-watcher too, when I was young. But my wife won't allow it now. Theatre-going, that's what she likes. And you'll understand the importance of compromise."

"Can you help me?"

"I won't make any promises. But if you return tomorrow with the certificate, I'll see what I can do."

"That would be wonderful." I thank him effusively.

As I leave I smile at the man at the counter, who pretends not to see me.

*　　　*　　　*

Theo and one of his friends carry the sofa indoors and plump themselves down on it. "Phew," Theo says. "Now for a cup of tea."

"I'll see what I can do."

I search in a packing box for tea, sugar and then cups. The house is cleaner than I remembered. But it's musty, dusty, a little too warm.

"I don't have any milk," I call into the room. It feels good, using my voice.

"Doesn't matter," they call back in chorus. I put the kettle on, and in the meantime empty one of the boxes. I realise I'm humming.

It's only when they've left that I notice the smell of the wooden floor—the dust sticks to my fingers. I take the clothes out of my suitcase, and then unpack the boxes with all the kitchen things. On the table that belonged to Theo's father I place my drawing paper, my books. I put the music stand in a corner by the window, where the light enters. I can keep an eye on the back garden from there: the small apple tree, the medlar, the large apple tree, the hedge.

I take my notebook out of doors to map my surroundings. First I make a sketch of the back garden, then the pear tree, its trunk entwined with ivy, the hazel tree and the oak that grows on the east side. To the west there is an apple tree, a currant bush, an elder and a bird cherry. In front of the house, on the side that faces the road, there's a little terrace, in an open space with two lawns, a may tree and a pergola. That's the best place for the bird table and the bird bath. By the hedge—overgrown with ivy—is the last of the apple trees, beside a plum and a small pear tree. There's enough fruit, at any rate, for a variety of birds. Around the garden are all kinds of hedges. It's the end of February. The experiment has begun.

The wind is still cold. I go inside to put on my coat and come back with a chair. I set it down on the terrace—it wobbles a little as I sit, the legs slipping on the round cobbles. There's a Great Tit in the hedge to my left, and a little later I see another one, or the same one, I'm not really sure—both have a broad stripe on their chests, so both are males. In the apple tree on the east side of the garden there are Magpies, in the plum tree a Wood Pigeon. There's rustling in the hedge, and a rainbow in the spider's web below the windowsill.

"Gwen?" Theo is at the gate. He grins and holds up a shopping bag. "Mary's sent me with some supplies. Because the shops are shut. We can't have you drinking tea without milk."

"How kind." I walk to the gate, avoiding the boggy patch, and take the bag.

He looks at my notebook. "What are you doing?"

I show him my sketch. "I'm going to study the birds who live here." He looks at the uneven circles that represent the trees. "My father was a bird lover too. In the spring we always took in a few baby Tits and Blackbirds who'd fallen from their nests or had been caught by cats."

He whistles. "That's a good idea. There are plenty of birds here and they're as bold as brass. There was a Great Tit, when Dad lived here, who'd fly right into the kitchen. But how will you research them?"

"I'm not sure yet. At any rate I want to win their trust. There's been a lot of research recently on bird intelligence, but in laboratories, and birds behave differently in captivity. It makes them nervous." A Pigeon lands in the apple tree. "I want to find out how they behave when they're free. And make a proper record of their song." I hope I can succeed— my ear is better trained now, but they sing so swiftly. And I have no idea if there'll be enough birds here for a serious study.

"Trust comes through the belly, for most animals." He pats his own belly, perhaps to show that he's an animal too, or simply to illustrate his point.

I ask him to thank Mary for me. In the kitchen I examine the contents of the bag: milk, bread, cheese, apples, potatoes, butter. I crumble a crust of bread onto a plate and add a few knobs of butter. I put the plate on the broad windowsill at the front of the house and sit down by the other side of the window. A Great Tit arrives almost immediately, and then another—so there were two of them. Then the Magpies come, screeching loudly, driving off the Great Tits. I wave my arm, but that startles all the birds. I'll have to think up a solution. And I need nesting boxes. Perhaps I can build some myself, or make them from old boxes and containers. One of the Great Tits returns. He scours the plate for the last crumbs, staying perched on the windowsill when he has finished. He's looking at me with his bright little eyes. "Hallo," I say.

*   *   *

A small black head, a mask that comes over the eyes, even blacker gleaming bead-eyes. White cheeks, black again beneath them, a little bib that turns into a stripe on the chest, running all the way down. A small yellow body, blackish-grey feet, wings that are black and blue, or greenish, or yellowish, depending on the light that falls on them—Thomas paints this kind of thing so well. A blue-white-black tail. In flight the underside of the wings is light grey, bluish grey, the tail edged with a white streak. The upper part of the back is yellowy green; the wings beneath are blue with white flashes; sometimes the yellow of the body is visible.

I'm sitting with my note pad in the shade of the oak tree. The Great Tit in the hedge keeps repeating the same little tune. The postman swings the gate open. "Morning, Miss Howard," he says at the top of his voice, to bridge the distance between us. "I've got a parcel for you."

The Great Tit is long gone.

"In future, could you please put all parcels in the post-box, at the top of the path?"

He looks offended. "Mr McIver used to be ever so pleased with my services. You see, if I put them in the post-box, they can get stolen or damaged by young rascals. I wouldn't advise it, but if you don't want the personal touch, that's up to you. The customer is always right."

"I'm sorry. It's because of the birds. I'm trying to win their trust." I show him my little book of notes and drawings, and try to explain what the plan is. He doesn't think much of this, but does seem to appreciate my taking the trouble to explain.

"So the post-box it is then. But wouldn't you like me to show when I've called? I can make very subtle signals." He wiggles his fingers a little, a subtle signal.

"No, thanks. But thank you for your understanding. And I'll put a sign on the post-box and by the path."

When he has left I make the signboards—paint on wood— two for the garden gates, one for the post-box and one for the path. That should be sufficient. When they're dry I hang them up with wire, the last one at the top of the path.

"So you're not in the mood for visitors any more?" Theo gives me a brown paper bag. "Mary has been baking bread, far too much for us." He is panting a little because of the uphill climb.

"I do like visitors, but the birds aren't so keen."

"Ah, they're henpecking you already."

"You're an exception, of course. You're always welcome. But maybe you could be a little quieter. Walk quietly. Don't call out. Perhaps they'll get used to you then."

He laughs. "Oh dear, I mustn't laugh either, of course." He laughs even louder as he walks away and I have to laugh too, in spite of myself.

I put the bread on the kitchen table and fill the kettle. Outside there is a piercing cheeping sound. One of the Blue Tits is perched in front of the window, looking at me. She's cheeping so loudly I can hear her through the glass. I go out and find her waiting by the door. She flies to the hedge by the old oak tree, then back to me, to the oak and again to me. I quicken my pace. At the oak I see her mate. He also seems distressed, flying swiftly back and forth over the hedge. The female swoops down. I kneel, see fragments of the nest, with its twelve eggs, spread across the ground beneath the nest box. The box is still intact, so I imagine that a cat has clawed the nest out—that means that I'll have to ensure that the boxes are more than six inches deep. I open the little box and put the nesting material back inside—first the shredded carton, then the moss and the horsehair. I carefully replace all the eggs, putting them against the back of the box so they're firmly positioned. When I've finished, the female immediately flies into the box and shifts the eggs to the centre. The male flies off, but quickly returns with an earwig in its beak. I stay watching them a moment, but the birds now ignore me. My fingers are tingling. They asked for help. I can hardly believe this happened.

*   *   *

Mown grass, low light, late summer; after some weeks of heat and no wind, a breeze is blowing. The air smells of autumn. I make a list of all the nests in the garden and write down who used which nest over the past year—the Blackbirds in the ivy, the Sparrows in the hedge (two pairs), the Great Tits in various trees. I walk along, checking everything, to make sure that nothing has been forgotten. I've given the regular birds their own names—I often mix them up still, but if they stay in one place for long enough, I can tell who is who. Their markings and colours are all a little different and each has its own way of moving, of reacting. Some birds are strident, and brisk in their movements, others almost merge into the background. I'm also beginning to recognise them by their song, both from their tunes and their voices. In London I perceived them as a group—there was an old Great Tit in the park whom I did recognise, and in the tree by Thomas's boat there was a pair we kept an eye on, but I had no idea that they differed so much from each other. Seeing requires time. In London there were too many distractions.

Theo has made a bird table for me, and every morning around half past six, when the day is still wet with dew, I put out a plate of food for them. Billy, a somewhat older male Great Tit, always comes first. He's quite bold, almost eating out of my hand already. He flies right up to my hand, takes a quick peck, then is off again, flying elsewhere. His wife is far shyer; I've called her Greenie, because the feathers on her back are much greener than those of the other birds. She does come to me, but only if Billy is there, and she flies off the moment I move. Birds are filled with air. They have various air sacs in their bodies and their bones are hollow. Air and light and swiftness.

I walk up the hill, past the hedge, to look for the nests there. Four brownish-grey rabbits are in the grassy field behind the house. They are quite still until they see me. Joan is getting married too. It's as if they all kept it at bay for so many years, and now they're grabbing their last chance. The green of the hedge, a few brown leaves, the green of the meadows. There is no end to this land; it simply merges into other land, another hill, and then into sea, always into the sea. I walk all the way to the end of the hedge, where the Henderson's gate cuts off the path. I take the long pathway back down the other side of the hill. In the graveyard behind the house I stumble over a tree root and fall hard onto my side. My notebook slides into a puddle of water. I immediately fish it out, but the notes have all run together. I remain sitting there for a moment. Perhaps it's a foolish idea, to study birds like this. Those scientists have studied for years, have read far more than me—perhaps I'll miss important details, make myself a laughing stock. If I write that the Blue Tit asked me for help, they'll accuse me of anthropomorphism, though I know for sure that it happened.

I stand up and brush the earth off my dark-red skirt. A grey squirrel with a silvery, almost translucent tail comes out of the hedge in front of my house. He looks at me for a moment, then bobs down to the ground, scampering swiftly back into the dark branches when I move my arm. If I don't make the attempt, I'll never know.

*   *   *

On the shortest day of the year, at the end of the afternoon, I find two Christmas cards in the red post-box, one from my sister, sending greetings from Mother and Dudley, and one from Thea in Canada. I put them on the table. I forgot to send cards myself—I've been much too busy. The Great Tits have started to enter the house, something that has required many practical adjustments. I have to clean the house daily and I've put all my precious possessions out of their way. I've put blankets on the sofa, and wash them every week. But perhaps I shouldn't use the sofa at all—I could replace it with a wooden bench with loose cushions. And the cold is getting harder to bear. During the day I leave the kitchen window and the top light in the sitting room open, so the birds can fly in and out. This afternoon I sat on the wooden chair by the window to study the types of natural food the birds choose in the winter, but even with an extra pullover and a rug across my knees I couldn't stand it for more than two hours. In the autumn it rained into the house for weeks on end; covering the windowsill with a plastic sheet was the only way to prevent it from going rotten.

The birds haven't only adapted to the house, but also to me. At first they would immediately fly outside whenever I moved, but now they keep a careful eye on what my body tells them. If I move gently, they stay where they are—this is how they've trained me into adjusting my own movements. They still startle if there are abrupt movements or unexpected noises, such as the telephone or the doorbell. There is a particular group of about eight Great Tits who are always visiting. Such darlings. The Sparrows are bossy, annoying characters; they drive away the other birds if they get half a chance. The Blue Tits are a little shyer than the Great Tits—they don't often allow themselves to be seen. Blackbirds sometimes visit, but generally go about their business. Up to now the Robins have only come as far as the windowsill. Last week a large male Great Tit came to the garden. He has a missing claw, as if he caught his foot in something. I call him Tiptoe. He doesn't ever get flustered, and this morning he came and sat on my hand a moment, while I was writing. His claws tickled. I was unable to hold my hand still for very long, so off he flew, at the first sign of movement.

I go and sit at the piano and play a few notes. Yesterday I heard one of the Blackbirds repeat a Bach motif. The back door blows open, then slams shut. On the table the top sheets of paper are blown off. The bird music. When I go to lock the door I see a figure by the path.

"Hallo?" No one answers. It must have been a ghost from the graveyard.

The wind increases: trees that before were sighing are now creaking. I don't know where all the creatures are, how they cope with this weather. I know so little. Greenie didn't come at all yesterday. I was afraid something had happened to her, but today she was here as usual. Sometimes I have the feeling that I'll never get a grip on it all. That I'll remain an outsider forever.

The house lets the wind in; there are gaps under the door, between the walls, in the window frames. We breathe with each other. The door was once a tree. I tap my fingers on the table, decide to make another cup of tea. After all, I won't be able to sleep in this weather.

The rose bush sweeps back and forth, from upright to almost flat on the ground. Branches swish. The bird table blows over, and the chair. The wind drowns the clatter.

Lightning. Silence. Crack.

I move the green chair to the window. The rain is now a constant stream of grey, blocking out the view. I can only see movement. Time is like movement; the grey gives this evening its shape. The word "evening" makes it seem that an evening is a specific thing, whereas every evening is different. Before was never like now.

The apple tree bends, cracks. I can't see whether a branch has broken off.

The rain forms a screen in front of the window. I could simply walk through it, into the garden, into the darkness, towards the future. To be surrounded by something greater than yourself, that is the dream of all mystics.

In the morning I take stock of the damage. The oak to the east of the house has lost a large bough, just like the apple tree by the hedge, but otherwise only twigs have broken off. The birds are calm and quiet, but there are fewer of them than usual. I don't know if they perhaps fled from the storm; I don't know where they could flee. I twice put food out on the bird table, for those who are still here—they certainly need an extra source of energy. Two strangers are visiting: a Robin and a Thrush. Perhaps the wind has blown them this way. The Thrush keeps its distance, the Robin copies the other Robins and goes to the bird table. It's often like that. Birds watch the behaviour of others of their kind to determine whether they're safe, if they can come closer. I move my hand, the Robin makes a little sideways hop, then immediately returns. He seems to be an oldish chap. The sky is blue; the night's oppressiveness has made way for feelings of relief. I go into the house. It's time to knead the dough, otherwise this afternoon's bread won't be ready.

STAR 10

In October Star came and perched on the windowsill again, using the pose that showed she wanted to tap. I was talking to Garth on the telephone. "Hang on a minute." I tapped five times, and held the receiver by the sill. She tapped five times in response. My friend was well able to hear it and reacted with enthusiasm. In the weeks that followed, Star and I continued to practise. The experiment made swift progress. Star never looked at me at all during the tapping and I am certain she reacted only to my voice; I made sure that I gave her no clues with my body.

In November I tried to interest other Great Tits in counting. Beauty, the son of Star and Baldhead, already liked to tap the lampshades. One quiet afternoon I tapped a couple of times against the shade with a pencil. He did not understand, flew away while I was tapping, then swiftly returned to fetch his peanut when I had finished. After that I tried Monocle. She did tap, but never the exact number I requested. She would generally give four taps and then very proudly come to ask for a nut. Star and Monocle had never again quarrelled after Baldhead's death, but Star became jealous if I was busy with another bird. Then she would sit somewhere close by and swiftly tap out the correct number.

In Nature I read about a study on Pigeons that showed they responded to instructions from the human voice. I decided to try this with Star. "Four," I said one morning and tapped four times. She tapped four too, and I gave her a nut. "Four," I said again. She kept looking at me. "Four." She hesitated, then bent forward and very swiftly tapped four times. We repeated this again later in the day: first by tapping at the same time as saying the word, and then with the word alone; she seemed to grasp the aim very well. In the weeks that followed she learned five, six, seven and eight in the same fashion. The number nine was not successful, because I could not tap it quickly enough. Time passes much more swiftly for birds than for human beings and my slow tapping probably bored Star. She always started to tap when I reached eight, so we never managed a higher number. This was our way of working that winter.

1943

The Canadians loom up from the mist, in the darkness of the coming winter, as if in a dream, something from former times. There are six of them, all heavily wrapped, their helmets an unnecessary ornament. The fellow in front is forcing his way through the hedge.

"Hey, hey, wait." I run out in my slippers. "You can't just do that."

A tall man steps forward. "We're on exercise, moving through the gardens into the town. We can't take account of the inhabitants."

The Great Tits have flown out of the hedge and they perch on me.

The man stares at me with his mouth half open, till I take a step forward. "Wow. I've been in England for years now, and I've never seen anything like this. I've never seen any wild birds behave like this. Anywhere."

I tell him about the birds that live here. That I'm researching them—their language, habits and individual characteristics. That birds are more sensitive to disturbance than people and that it took years to build this trust. Trust precedes friendship, precedes every close relationship, but it grows deeper if it isn't betrayed.

"So this isn't an English custom? You just decided to live with these birds?" He takes off his helmet.

"The Great Tits decided to live in the house with me."

Patch flies towards me, hesitates, but then lands on my head.

"Amazing. Never seen birds so tame before." He leans towards me to take a better look. Patch flies away. "Listen, we'll change our plans. A little tricky, but we'll have to do it. Pay attention, guys." The men listen less carefully than the Great Tits. He tells them to bypass the garden. The fellow in the hedge is still stuck there. His leader gives him a look, warning him to take care.

As soon as the men start moving, the birds fly up, into the chestnut tree, into the hedge, across the field—to understand the world like this, from a tree, from within a hedge. I can hear the men talking a little longer, laughing, their leader explaining something to them with his deep voice.

The next afternoon I see that the signboard at the top of the path has vanished. I thought I heard soldiers this morning—and now they have a souvenir, something tangible to back up their tall stories. Now there's no signboard there, and perhaps that's better. A sign attracts people's attention, and what the birds most need is peace and quiet.

*   *   *

Black Geese form a V against the white sky. Barbed wire, light mist. I knock, nudge open the back door of the farmhouse, explain the situation, ask as politely as I can.

The woman at the table shakes her head. "I'm sorry." She drops a potato into the pan of water and takes another from the sack in front of her on the table.

I thank her and leave. There's no butter anywhere now. Not in Keymer, nor in Westmeston, and probably not in Clayton either. I've called at all the farmhouses, but everything has already been taken for the soldiers and quantities are checked. I would be able to manage with the set ration, but it's not enough for the birds. They say it's going to be a cold winter and I lost too many Tits last year already.

I walk south along Brighton Road, to Clayton Hill. I would really like to call at one last farmhouse, but my feet are on fire. Moreover, if I walk back via Keymer, I won't manage to get home before ten. The long, empty fields seem blue; the hedges that divide them are bare. Sheep stand with their backs towards me. They've forecast rain, says Theo. He has the radio on all day. Yesterday he said that he thought he should enlist, even though he's exempt.

A jeep approaches me from behind. I keep close to the hedge. As it passes I see there are four soldiers inside. The driver brakes and then reverses, the sound of the engine higher and louder than just now.

When he reaches me, he leans out. I don't stop. He drives beside me at walking pace. "Can we give you a lift?"

"No, thanks. And besides, I wouldn't fit."

The men at the back whoop. No, not men, they're boys, spotty, pimply, barely out of school.

"They'll budge up for you, miss. Aw, come on. We'll do you a fry-up, at the camp." A wink, laughter, elbow prods.

"Sorry, chaps."

The man at the wheel shrugs. "Okay. Up to you." His voice is raw and smoky, growling above the engine.

All four of them wave at me, children on an outing. I wave back and grin, in spite of myself. On the other side of the road I spot a large bird and hold my breath—a Goshawk.

The path up the hill is muddy. A little stream runs down its centre, over the gravel. I choose the water rather than the clods of mud, hoping that the soles of my boots are high enough. A brown horse looks over the fence at me. I say hallo, then hear a Spotted Woodpecker to my left. A Robin rustles in the hawthorn. A Wagtail flies up as I walk past. The wood begins a few yards further up—I can hear an Owl—last week I saw a Barn Owl in the garden. It wasn't a warm year, there won't be enough mice for them.

Dusk settles down among the trees. Blue turns to bluey-grey, ten minutes, dark bluey-grey, twenty, I walk downhill, dark grey against black. I only see my boots because they're walking, I only walk because there is a rhythm, I follow the rhythm of my feet and move automatically.

At the gate I look for the key to my post-box, the little flag has been raised. The keys are under my purse, at the bottom of my shopping basket. I find them by touch. The lock of the post-box is rusty. I jiggle at it; it takes a while to get it open. Two letters.

"Gwen?"

A tall, bearded man is standing by the oak tree. I haven't seen him for more than twenty years, but I recognise Paul immediately.

*   *   *

I walk ahead of him, on the path up to the house. My heart is beating so loudly—if he walked closer, he'd hear it. He stays behind me, step by step. "Are you all right?"

He clears his throat. "Yes. But it's cold." Foxes are yipping in the distance.

I open the door—the key trembles in my hand—and turn on the light inside. "Sit down." I indicate the armchair by the hearth. "I'll make a pot of tea. And would you like something to eat?" He's shivering. I take his coat, heavy and stiff with dirt. Once he's sitting in the chair, covered with a blanket, I light the fire.

He gives a faint smile and gazes at the flames. I sort out the bed in the guest room. I mustn't forget to give him a hot-water bottle. Peetur comes to take a look and flies with me from my shoulder to the linen cupboard.

"You must think it's strange," he says. I hand him a cup of tea with plenty of sugar and a slice of cake on the saucer. "Me standing at your door, without warning." His eyes are dull.

"I'm sorry, there's no milk. I swop milk for butter, for the Tits and Robins and occasional Sparrow. Milk's no good for them."

"I've walked all the way." He dips the cake into his tea. "You're still busy with birds, are you?" He finishes the cake in three mouthfuls.

"You'll have to behave yourself, you know. They're not keen on strangers."

"And your violin? Come on, play something for the weary traveller." His shoes are wet.

"Take off your shoes. I'll fetch some socks." Socks, bread—and butter, but never mind—another cup of tea. His feet are all red, covered in sores and blisters, craters, hills, all red and white—a miniature landscape of war. He puts the socks on, pulls the blanket up to his armpits.

"Goodness, Gwennie. You're all grown up now!"

I laugh. "You too."

He shuts his eyes as I tune my violin. Something light—I play Satie for him, making it sound like an evening: blue, but clear, and not too melancholic.

Meanwhile the fog wraps itself around the house, thicker and thicker, till you can't see beyond your own hand; the arm simply stops at the elbow and the trees recede gently, tree by tree by tree. The Great Tits have gone to their roosts already, not at all disturbed by the man in the blanket who is simply breathing now, not thinking any more, drifting in and out of sleep as I play—in, out, in, out—till the day turns to night. Till it's completely silent outside, and the sky is dark grey and heavy.

The next morning he's already up when I get out of bed. I can hear footsteps move into the kitchen, hear him open the window—someone must be on the windowsill. He comes into the sitting room, starts to make the fire. I can't have that. We'll run out of wood soon. I stand. "Paul, I never light the fire during the day. Otherwise we won't get through the winter."

"I'll chop some wood for you." His voice sounds deeper than before, warmer. Perhaps my memory has distorted its sound. I used to love his voice.

He sits down in the armchair. Hop and Skip watch him from the lamp stand. "Aren't they tame!"

"I've worked at it. They know now that they have nothing to fear from me." I tell him about my research, that I some-times write articles on birds for two different magazines about country life: *Out of Doors and Countrygoer* and *Countryman*. I'd like to write for a proper scientific journal, but they don't take my work seriously. "And what about you?"

He tells me that he joined the Forces, the Air Transport Auxiliary. He'd had previous experience of flying and they needed older pilots to ferry the planes, sometimes even to the Continent. He was short of cash, had problems with his lady friend—it seemed the ideal solution. It went well at first, but was hazardous; they were under continual threat of attack from the Germans, even when flying over England. But one dark Tuesday evening he met a girl, big dark eyes, a green frock, a soft laugh. He went back to her parents' farm with her. It was easy, like clockwork almost. The next morning he woke up in the hay barn. Alone and too late for his flight. One of his friends, Simon, knew about the girl and flew instead of him. The plane was shot down over the Channel. Paul falls silent. Hop swoops down from the lamp to the table, looking for crumbs in the thick chenille. "I couldn't do a damned thing to stop it. When I got to base, I was immediately hauled before the CO. Someone had apparently said that I'd passed information to the Hun. I denied this at once, of course. They asked for proof. But everyone knows that innocence is hard to prove. I told them about the girl, so they questioned her, but she denied it all. Frightened of her father, I think. Or perhaps it was a trap."

"Why do you think so?"

"I don't know, it just feels wrong. I'd never missed a flight before." He taps his forefinger on the arm of the chair.

Hop finds something in the tablecloth and flies out of the window with it.

"Two weeks back there was a bit of a scuffle as they were exercising the prisoners, and I was able to escape. I hid in an empty cabin in the woods, and when the food ran out, I went on the tramp. I thought of your father. He was always good to me."

Father always saw Paul as more of a son than Kingsley or Duds.

"Someone told me that your sister is taking care of your Mother and Dudley. They live in Budleigh Salterton, right?"

I nod. "Newman died in 1936, of pneumonia." It's been a long time since I thought about my father. I pinch my thigh.

"And your older brother?"

"Kingsley stayed in France after the First World War. We thought he'd been lost in action, but in 1919 he wrote a letter to say that he'd met someone and that the girl already had his child."

"In the Forces then, like me."

My mother visited him in France once. She didn't say much about it, just that he had a darling wife, and two darling children. "Darling"—a word cast over things to soften them. Hop flies in again, straight to the chenille cloth. He pecks at it as if it's a lawn.

"And then I heard you were living alone in Ditchling. Closer than Devon, and with the advantage that just one person would know that I'm here."

"So, you're not here for me, then." It's a joke, not a reproach.

"You haven't let me finish what I was saying." He sounds offended. "And that person would be you. I know you found me attractive, in the past—but you were still too young. I shouldn't have had that fling with Margaret. I know it broke your heart."

"Don't overrate yourself." That day by the water—the heat, the boat, the wet chemise. "Margie has lived in France for years too, with her husband."

"And didn't you ever marry?"

I shake my head. Thomas sent me a letter last year, saying he missed me. It's in the top drawer of my desk. Skip flies out. Hop follows him, tries to overtake him at the top window, veers sharply at the last moment so as not to fly against the pane. A few tiny feathers lie on the table. I pick them up and put them in the drawer, with the other feathers. It's a shame to throw them away.

"And what are your plans?"

"I'd hoped to stay here a while. To catch breath." He looks questioningly at me. I bide my time. "And then I'll go north. I have a friend who lives in Scotland, with his parents."

There is no plan. "How long is a while?"

"A week?" He searches my face for clues. "A few days?"

"A week is fine. I'm afraid I don't have enough supplies for any longer."

He nods, barely. "I'll sort out my own food."

"You're not going to sort out anything at present. Just rest a while. But how's Patricia?"

"She's divorced. Living in London and working for a small publishing firm." He says she's living with a woman and is much happier now. "I'll tell her you said hallo."

I give a whistle as I put food on the bird table and realise that I'm doing this because the birds are avoiding me. "Sorry,"

I say to Star, all bright and cheery. She then lands on my shoulder and hops down to my open hand for her peanut.

That afternoon, after cleaning the house, I walk to the Alfords' farm across the fields behind Bird Cottage. My boots leave prints in the wet grass, carry mud along, then drop it again a little further on. Sink, tug. The Alfords have dairy cows and if Mrs Alford isn't there, I can perhaps buy some butter or cheese. The Great Tits follow me, flitting around my head. Little Michael is playing in the sandpit in front of the house.

"Is your Daddy at home?"

He nods, runs inside. The birds fly to the hedge.

"Hullo, Gwen." Michael senior's face seems more furrowed than normal.

"How are you?" I ask. In the air above the meadow Starlings are dipping and diving in formation together— opening, closing, circling.

He tells me that his wife has been ill all week. The doctor is coming tomorrow.

"Do you have enough food?"

"Food isn't the problem." He takes me to the cowshed. "Sit down, won't you?" The breathing of the cows helps me relax, their warmth briefly embraces me. "We simply don't earn enough. I can't pay the doctor with coupons."

Little Michael comes into the shed with a drawing. "It's a Great Tit!"

"Very good!" A triangle protrudes from a circle—that must be the beak—and there's a pair of little twigs for the legs.

As I begin to return the drawing, he tells me I can keep it.

"He's always watching the birds," his father says. "And he's very keen on the Swallows." They nest in the byre here each summer. Alford is planning to sell his cows, so how much longer will the Swallows come?

He fetches a piece of butter, wraps it in brown paper. "This is all I have."

I thank him profusely and tuck it into my bag with the drawing. Little Michael comes out with me. When I stretch my arms, the Great Tits fly from the hedge and perch on my arms and head. Michael imitates me and looks very crestfallen when they don't come to him. Then he pretends to be a bird, flying in front of me to the field with the sheep, over the gate, running ahead with widespread arms till we reach the cemetery. Then he circles a few times. "And now fly away home," I say.

*   *   *

Night-time, his breath against my cheek, then the brush of his lips. I don't stop him, but don't turn my face to him either.

"Len." He takes my arm.

I step aside, shake his arm off.

"Come on." He takes my hand, opens the door to the bedroom.

I shake my head and give a light smile. I squeeze his hand a moment, release it, then enter my bedroom.

The birds are already sleeping. The sheets are damp. I really ought to have a fire in the bedroom too. I hear Paul enter the guest room. It's windy outside, branches lashing.

The guest-room door opens again. He goes to the lavatory, urinates. I pull up the blanket that lies at the foot of the bed. His footsteps sound in the passage, then go silent, but the door doesn't open. It starts to rain. Drops tap softly against the windowpane, then louder. Then I hear the door after all, slow steps, the creaking bed.

The shadow of the tree by the window crosses the curtain, sends an echo across the ceiling, over the blanket. Over me under the blanket. I pinch the sheet. Shadows roam the room. I don't know how long it takes before I fall asleep.

Poppy wakes me by pulling a hair out of my head. I shake her off, then swing my legs out of the bed. There is more light than there has been these past few days; the rain has moved on. The sun shines behind wispy grey clouds. It's almost December. Perhaps there is no friend in Scotland. I put food on the table for the birds, smell winter in the morning air. They're all here: Hop, Skip, Dodie, the other Great Tits, the Blackbirds.

Paul is wearing the clothes I've washed for him. "Can I hang on to this pair of socks?"

"Of course. Take another pair too. And will you write, when you get there?"

He smiles and avoids my gaze. "I will." Words don't mind what they're used for.

Hop lands on the kitchen cupboard, takes a quick look, and then flies off. Dodie replaces him. She makes eye contact with me, then looks at Paul, and flies away. "They're not used to it," I say.

Paul turns his head. "Who?"

"The birds. They're not used to other people."

"They sing beautifully."

"Some are more gifted than others. Peetur invents his own songs, often entirely new ones, though his favourite call is 'Pee-tur. Pee-tur.' Patch only sings the simplest phrases."

He makes breakfast. We eat together in silence. The soft bread sticks to the roof of my mouth—the roof, the canopy. I tell him to eat an extra slice of bread, force him to do so by buttering it for him. It would be a shame to waste it now. The Great Tits fly back and forth; they're always restless when winter is on the way. They only settle down when it's really cold. Before that they're busy with their preparations, storing food for the winter.

I slice bread for him, put some apples on the table, and a piece of cheese. He silently packs his knapsack. He could stay; we could stay together.

His back in front of the window, a silhouette against the light.

I give him the food, tell him at which farm he can get milk and hand him my coupons.

"I haven't chopped wood for you yet."

"I'll do that myself." My voice is light. Light as deal wood, suitable for making a light table.

I embrace him, not too long, then open the door. As he walks down the pathway, the sun breaks through. The wind is blowing from the south. I can smell the sea.

He turns one more time and waves. I call his name, tell him to wait, his face lights up, I run towards him, stop a moment when I reach him, gently touch his arm, his cheek, then snuggle into his arms, into his kiss, ask him to stay. Here. He walks back to the house with me. I kiss him again as we're walking and it's not quite right yet, but it will be fine—

No. He turns one more time and waves. I raise my hand, turn round and go into the cottage, to the kitchen, where I put the kettle on and have to wipe the tears from my eyes to see the mug I want to get from the cupboard. Patch flies into the cupboard. I don't laugh, but drive him out with my hand, not hard, but it gives him a shock. "Sorry," I say. "Sorry, little one."

STAR 11

When spring came, Star again built a nest with Peetur. But when the nestlings were three weeks old fate struck: Peetur disappeared. I never saw him again. I think the neighbour's ginger cat must have caught him: it would lurk in the lavender bush near the nest, hungrily eyeing the little ones. After that Star took care of her brood alone and did so marvellously.

After Peetur vanished, a stranger came into Star's territory. She already had her work cut out with finding food for her young, and his presence made her nervous. I helped her as much as I could but I could not keep watch for her all the time. The stranger drove all the other male Great Tits from the garden and then tried to court Star. He would perch outside her nest box, always singing the same three notes. Star pretended not to notice him. He tried all kinds of tricks to attract her attention, even mimicking her call note, a distinctive double-noted call, with the consequence that she never used that call again. The most annoying thing was that he ate so much food, most of the insects and seeds that the garden provided. I made sure she had extra provisions and every time she came to me I gave her a peanut, but Star preferred to give natural food to her young.

On 30th May the first four fledglings flew the nest; the next day the other three followed. But these were really too young to fly and remained in the grass under the old oak. Star fiercely defended them: there was a Sparrow she wanted to drive off, and she struck so much fear into him that he flew off in utter panic. Serve him right! Those wretched Sparrows think they rule the roost. The smallest fledglings did not survive, however, and two days after their death Star took the remaining youngsters to the garden on the other side of the lane, where there was sufficient cover, out of the range of the Stranger Great Tit, in whom she was clearly not interested at all. She did continue to return to me for food, however.

That spring our bond grew closer and she became very fond of me, perhaps because she had lost her mate. Baldhead had died the previous year, and now Monocle was the only one of the old guard remaining, and Star had never been very friendly with her. The moulting season started in July. Star still did not roost inside the house, but often sought my company during the day. In mid-August she began to behave a little strangely: she would ruffle up her feathers, as if she wanted to drive me off. Because we had never started our counting earlier than September, I did not realise that this had something to do with our experiment, until one morning she clearly adopted the posture that she always employed to tell me that she wanted to tap. I tapped twice on the wood, and, lo and behold, she immediately tapped back, very excited, because I had finally grasped what she meant.

1944

"Gwennie!" My sister is standing on the platform, waving as if she's about to drown.

"How good to see you." I give her a hug. The skin of her face is as baggy as an old lady's and she has a different smell. Her blonde hair is almost white. "Aren't you well?"

She frowns. "Why do you ask?" Her fingers close around my wrist.

"You're so thin."

"There's a war on, Gwen. Lucky for you that there's still food where you live."

"We'll soon be home." It's a good half-hour walk from Hassocks Station.

The sky is ash grey, the world is so vast. There's a thin layer of ice on the path beside the railway line. The grass crunches beneath our feet. The sole of Olive's left shoe is loose. "Would you like to wear my shoes?"

"No." Her voice is faint; she's out of breath, though we're not walking all that fast. "Nice, these hills here."

"If we have the time, we could go for a walk, to Ditchling Beacon"—the old lookout post—I'm not sure she'll manage it.

She links her arm in mine and tells me that Dudley caught pneumonia when it was so rainy last autumn. And Mother doesn't know where she is sometimes and who Olive is. "She doesn't drink any more, though. That's one good thing about the war. There still was more than enough gin in the first year, but thrift was never her strongest point. She's been in a rotten mood for three years now."

I laugh. "And what about you? How did things turn out with Timothy?"

"After we left Wales, we wrote to each other for a while. But in 1940 he moved to Manchester with his wife. That's where she's from, and her parents had wanted her there for a long time already. We haven't been in touch since." Her eyes are clouded, misted glass.

"Do you miss him?" A Blackbird flies from the hazel tree, a stranger.

She shakes her head. "We have two little girls living with us now, six and eight years old. Evacuees, from London. They're sweet kids, but very poor. Their cardies were in absolute tatters when they came to us. But we got them new outfits, of course. They adore the garden, with the hens and all the birds. And when there's no school, which is often, I take them for little walks. When they first came they couldn't tell the difference between a Sparrow and a Great Tit! And they love the beach. They can spend hours looking for clams and cockles and razor shells."

We're walking past the meadow where the White-fronted Geese graze. They fly up when we come too near. They're growing increasingly timid because each year more of them are shot.

When we reach the church she wishes to climb up to it—it's on a hill, and there's an old graveyard with a view over Lewes Road and South Street, all the way to the Downs.

"Swallows nest here in the summer. Baby Swallows are my favourite birds—they're so playful!" Knowing the world through flight, mapping the land below, being light enough for that.

"Oh, you can see so far from up here." She's gasping for breath.

I point to the Anne of Cleves House on the other side of the street, which Henry VIII granted her when they divorced. We go down the steep steps back to the road and then walk across it. I take the suitcase from her. Her hand is cold, bony. She really is very thin. She holds herself like an old woman. I'm old too. Since Paul left, I haven't had my monthly period. We walk the last section in silence. The air smells of fire—perhaps they're burning rubbish somewhere. In the pine tree opposite the cottage something or someone is rustling. Last week I spotted a Buzzard here.

When we're inside I make up the fire—it's evening now, and winter. I give her the slice of cake that Mary gave me. She wolfs it down. "There'll be bread and soup later. I know it's not much."

"It's more than we have." She takes a last large bite. "All these bird boxes in your bedroom. Papa would have liked that." In the past Olive would have called them filthy. She closes her eyes, turns her face to the warmth of the fire.

"Paul was here, you know. For a few days. At the end of last year. He'd had problems in the Air Force. He went north, afterwards, to a friend. He was going to let me know when he arrived. But I never heard anything else from him at all."

Olive opens her eyes, a little wider than usual, sweeping her gaze like a searchlight across my face. "Haven't you heard, then?"

"Heard what?"

"He was a traitor. They caught him in January, put him in prison in London, then executed him."

I take a deep breath.

"It was in all the papers."

Everyone knows that innocence is hard to prove. My face is burning. All sensation has left the rest of my body. Olive touches my arm. "I'm sorry. I didn't realise that you two were still in touch. Otherwise I'd have let you know." Hop swoops in and then immediately out again when he sees that the lamp is lit. They don't like artificial light.

He could have chopped wood. No one needed to know anything about it. I shake my head. The light is still crumbling in fragments in front of me; in the fire a piece of wood breaks apart.

*   *   *

The Alfords had no milk, or butter, or cheese. We walk silently along Spatham Road to the next farmhouse. The trees at the side of the road are bare, hard lines against the grey sky. No birds in sight.

Olive walks with her shoulders hunched forward, head down, a weary donkey. Trees become bushes, then fields, then trees again. The clouds in the distance are almost black.

"It's not going to rain, is it?" Her voice sounds croaky.

"I couldn't say."

"You knew I was coming to visit, didn't you? Why couldn't you sort this out before?"

"What do you mean?"

She gestures towards the farms in the distance. "There's enough to eat here, surely?"

I tell her there's barely enough, and that I'm always having to hunt out food for the birds too. She gives me a fierce look, like the vixen whom I accidentally disturbed in her den last summer.

"Olive, are you happy, living with Mother and Dudley?"

"What kind of a question is that?" She stands still. "It's easy enough for you, apparently, to abandon people. That's not how I am."

I start walking again and she follows. "It's normal for children to lead their own lives."

"Easily said, for you."

"I haven't abandoned anyone."

That look again. "You never visit. It was really difficult for Mother, that you went away. And someone has to look after Dudley."

The sky grows darker. I quicken my pace. Olive lags behind. I take her arm. "We have to hurry now. The next farm is still quite far away."

*   *   *

The morning has made the grass wet. Dewdrops slide across my toecaps. I wave at the train until it's out of sight. Olive has taken two bags of food away with her. We spent all yesterday trekking to farms and orchards. She's wearing my best shoes. I do hope that Olive's visit hasn't disturbed the birds too much. The coming months won't be easy for them. A truck drives past, soldiers, hooting. I raise my hand and wave them away.

A traitor. I raise my coat collar. He lied, about that friend in Scotland, and I knew he was lying and that's why I didn't want him to stay. Because he'd lied to me before. If he'd been straight with me, he could have stayed. Perhaps I should go and visit the girl he was talking about, work out what really happened. And I should write to Patricia too.

There are two boys by the pond—schoolboys, no older than ten. They're hurling stones.

"Stop that at once!" I stride firmly towards them.

The smaller one pulls his cap over his forehead. "Why, miss?"

"You should be ashamed of yourselves. Throwing stones at the Moorhens."

"We're just skimming stones," the bigger one stammers.

"If you two don't stop, and quickly, I'll let your parents know and then you'll be for it!"

"But we're not throwing stones at the birds."

The Moorhens are on the other side of the pond, hiding among the reeds, keeping a careful eye on us.

At the end of the street I turn around to check. The boys are still by the pond. It does indeed look as if they're skimming stones.

I tap at the shop window and give a wave. Theo beckons me to come in. "Cup of tea, Gwen? It's so cold. Has your sister gone home now?" He listens to the radio a little longer before switching it off.

"I've just brought her to the train."

"Sit down." The shop feels empty. Theo's stock has dwindled by at least half. He gave Olive soap, tea and flour to take home with her. Too much, really. She'd have protested if she hadn't needed it so badly.

EVA MEIJER

I pick at a hangnail. Old skin by an old fingernail, dead matter.

"They're saying that the Germans have lost half their troops already. That it's just a question of time."

"That would be good. I can hardly get enough butter for the birds. And without that, my research can go to blazes." I'm writing an article about bird intelligence for *Out of Doors and Countrygoer*.

"Gwen, millions have died on the Continent. Ordinary people. Children. I don't want to deny the importance of your research, but what's happening there is of an entirely different order." He pours the tea, adds sugar, and a drop of milk. He looks up at me. "And birds have survived cold winters before now. They'll cope."

I lift the cup from the saucer, blow on the tea.

"Is something the matter?"

"Olive told me that a friend of mine has been executed. A good friend. From long ago. A poet. He was a traitor, or so they say. I just can't imagine it."

"The war does strange things to people." He shrugs. A fact of life. These things happen. Even to the best of us.

"I was in love with him. When I was a girl. But he preferred my cousin. She was a real heartbreaker."

"Would you like another cuppa?" Because that always makes things better.

I shake my head. "How are Mary and the children?"

"Linda has a cough, and Timmy has too much energy." He laughs. "I'll be happy when the winter's over and I can throw them out of the house again. Mary too."

While we're talking a Sparrow lands on the windowsill,

not one I know. He pecks at the dry leaves that are piled by the window frame—perhaps there are little beasties there. I tell him about Olive, that she's taken over my father's role in the household.

"Until last week I didn't even know you had a sister. It's odd though, that they've stuck together like that, and you completely went your own way."

"Olive didn't dare to leave." I push the cup away from me. "And she didn't want me to leave either. My mother used to have my dresses made too small for me, because she adored tiny waists. I always felt that I had to hold my breath."

Dusk covers the land. I ask him to say hallo to Mary from me, then put on my coat. The thought of Paul hovers around me, like a ghost, the presence of an absence.

"Never say die, Gwen," Theo says, giving me a thumbs up, a nudge in the right direction, helping me on my way.

The wind carries me further. I walk into the darkness—the hill, the blueness that deepens around me. At home the Great Tits are already seeking out their roosting places. I take up my violin, search for something challenging, Bartok, my fingers slow, my body a rusty machine. All the music is still stored inside it, just a little further off than before.

Loss is understanding that nothing was ever yours.

Grief is understanding that hope has vanished, or not quite understanding it yet.

STAR 12

On 10th September Star perched on the armrest of the green chair with her head pointing down, a sign that she wanted to tap. I went to the window frame with her, where I tapped four times and she imitated me. The next day Dado came by, just when we wanted to begin. Dado and Star were constantly squabbling about the territory within the trees to the west of the cottage. Dado had a mate, Presto, and therefore, according to bird law, she was higher in the pecking order than Star, who had no mate at all. So Dado had the right to chase her away whenever she wanted. Dado flew at Star on the windowsill, then at me, but I would not let her intimidate me and called for Star, who immediately returned. I gave her a nut, then she flew out of the window. Half an hour later she returned for a tapping session, moving her tail restlessly back and forth, as a signal to the Great Tits in the room next door. She was afraid they would prevent her from doing her work. On the following day Star stayed out of doors. I tapped on the armrest of the garden bench, but that startled her and she flew swiftly away. Great Tits use tapping as a way to drive off other birds and Star was not used to tapping outside with me. She would always raise her head feathers when she tapped for me, to signal that the tapping was part of our experiment and that she did not wish to drive me away.

In the last week of September the Great Tits began to tear paper again and to tap against the lampshade in the sitting room, something that really distracted Star. Our sessions grew shorter and were often interrupted. Moreover she was still bothered by Dado, as well as by the Nameless Intruder who had returned to the garden again. One afternoon

Monocle came to take a look at what we were doing. Star found her presence annoying and tapped four rather than five. I gave Monocle a peanut to encourage her to fly out of the house, which is exactly what happened. Star immediately wanted to continue with the tapping. Previously it had made her jealous if I gave another bird a nut before she received her own, but now the tapping itself had become important for her. That autumn she displayed no interest in the male birds and during the counting was much more concentrated than before. She now wanted to count whenever we saw each other.

1949

Silver light, sun through the mist. The field doesn't end, it becomes soft grey then turns into sky. The birds were late this morning: at half past seven Tessa was still in her roosting box. The chill envelopes my skin. I'm shivering. Yesterday I knew for certain that it would be misty today. Yet only a few months ago the birds could still surprise me—because, for example, they were so intently searching for food, then on the next day rainy weather would set in for three weeks. Or they'd stick close to the house one morning, and later there'd be a storm. Last week, however, I realised it was suddenly going to turn hot. Perhaps I can read the weather better now because I've lived longer here, but I think I've learned this skill from the birds. Or I can see it in their behaviour, without exactly knowing how.

At the bird table Star comes and perches on my shoulder. I give her a peanut from my apron pocket. I want her to come inside soon, to be photographed. But all Great Tits are afraid of strangers. I've told the photographer that I can't make any promises.

I put some more food on the bird table to tempt them— bread, bacon, cheese, raisins.

"Hallo!" It's Roger, from the well-known journal *British Birds*, with his camera tucked beneath his brown herringbone coat. His dark eyebrows are wet with mist.

"I thought Joseph would be coming too."

"He'll be here later. His train was delayed. And I didn't want to make you wait." He smiles his lopsided smile. "And mornings are better for the birdies, right?"

The birdies. I smile, trying not to let my irritation show. Joseph is quite different, not so false.

"Would you like tea? Do sit." I gesture towards the table.

He wipes the chair with his hand before sitting. "I've had a word with the editorial team. We've had excellent responses to the piece you sent to us about birdsong. We'd like to make the following proposal: we'll hold the interview today, and that will appear in next week's issue; and then you'll have a series of eight articles to follow. Then, if both sides are satisfied, we could extend the agreement."

I put a cup of tea down for him. This is for the birds, I'm doing this for the birds, I mustn't spoil things by getting irritated.

"That seems a very good idea." Another smile, and that's quite enough.

We discuss deadlines and my fee, and then Joseph arrives, panting, face flushed, hair damp against his head.

"Sorry, I got lost, because of the fog. I ended up behind your house, at your neighbour's, and she brought me to the top of your path as I was so disorientated. Left, right, couldn't tell the difference any more. Oh good, a cup of tea. Nice to see you, Gwendolen. Excellent article on variation in birdsong. We were all so impressed. Sorry, I'm babbling. But phew am I glad to be here!"

Bluebeard flies in and straight out again at the sight of my guests.

The first questions are about the Great Tits. I explain that after a few weeks they realised I wouldn't harm them, and then they came into the house of their own accord. Joseph is humming, making notes. "But what exactly brought you here?" He brushes a lock of hair from his eyes.

"Is that important?"

"Our readers will be curious to know."

"I've always had an interest in birds. My father used to rescue baby birds that had fallen from their nests, and bring them home with him. We even had a tame Crow once." Charles. Could he still be alive, perhaps?

Joseph continues his questions, and brick by brick my answers build a wall around me, all neatly mortared. He has his own camera ready, and when Star lands on my shoulder, snaps a photo.

"Look, one of the Tits," Roger cries out, waving his arm around, at which Star swiftly flies away.

"I think we're almost done now," I say.

Roger stands. He walks across to my bed, examines the roost boxes on the picture rail above it, takes a photo of them. My bedroom, their bedroom. I look at Joseph. He shrugs. Roger proceeds through the whole house like this. Indignation flushes through my body, like a fever.

"He's driving them all away."

"I'll come alone some time. He doesn't realise what he's doing." He gives me a pat on the shoulder. "Anyway, we should go now. I have two more interviews today. Roger?" He calls into the passage. "Roger?"

The passage is empty. He's at the kitchen sink, camera at the ready like a gun. Bertie is on the curtain rod, stiff with shock.

"It's all right, Bertie," I say. "He'll soon be gone." I position myself between Roger and the bird. "He is afraid of you."

Bertie is very attached to me. He's a timid little bird with a penetrating gaze.

"Hang on. I've almost got him. I just need to get a little closer."

"No. That's enough now."

He steps sideways, past me, sticks his camera in the air, stumbles on a chair leg, and falls right over the chair with his clumsy body. Bertie cheeps, recoils even further, steps off the rail, startles, and gets stuck between the curtain rod and the wall.

"Are you happy now?" I ask quietly, trying not to make things worse. I push him aside and go and fetch the kitchen steps from the hall cupboard. Stay where you are, little one, otherwise you'll break something. "Get that man out of here," I tell Joseph.

I climb up the steps and take hold of Bertie, who fortunately does not resist. "Come on then, little chap." His wings are folded round his body. I cup it with my left hand, while with my right I feel under the curtain rod to see where he's caught and then I push him up. The trick is to shape your hands into a little hollow around the bird's body, but without any force or pressure; if birds know they can't move they give in, and if they can't sense any force they don't resist. Roger is taking photos. I come down from the steps and check Bertie's feet—nothing seems to be broken—and the wings are whole too. His heart is beating very quickly and he's making a soft little peeping noise that I've never heard him make before. I put him inside a box. He needs time to recover.

"Off with you," I tell Roger. "And I want to see the photos before publication."

"Right you are, Gwen," Joseph says. He gives a swallow and fumbles at his jacket.

Trembling, I open the door for them. This really is the last time, the very last time, that I'll allow strangers to visit. Theo, Mary, Garth, no one else will ever come inside again.

The telephone rings. I walk to the sitting room. There are no birds in sight.

"It's Garth. How was it, Gwen?"

"Awful. Joseph is nice enough, but Roger—what a conceited pig." I tell Garth about him taking Bertie's photo and about the fall.

Garth gives a hesitant laugh. "Sorry," he says. "I realise it's very unpleasant for you, and particularly for the birds, but I can really picture it." He laughs louder. "And you just shoving him aside."

I laugh too, in spite of myself. That silly fool.

When I hang up the house is silent—too silent. I call Star, and then Baldhead, but they don't come. It was a mistake to invite these people here. Vanity. That interest in my personal life, what use is that to the birds? I call Star again. But I do want people to learn about birds, so they can understand them better, treat them better. For years now the number of garden birds has been declining. Some species have almost vanished because people don't lay out their gardens correctly. And the ideas people have about birds are often wrong. But perhaps I'm deceiving myself. Perhaps the birds really don't get anything from this at all.

*   *   *

Rosy skies, red skies. I put a plateful of food on the bird table and go indoors to fetch a cardigan—it's still cold in the mornings. By the time I return they're already flying back and forth. They're all here: Bluebeard, Monocle, Baldhead, Star, Tinky, Tipsy, the young birds, Teaser and Peetur from the last brood, and over there Monocle and Tinky's youngsters, who have only just fledged. I drink my tea sitting on the bench. Tinky perches by me a moment, the fledglings fly right over my head and back, and then do the same again. Tinky sings a few notes to Monocle, who ignores him because she's busy eating.

"Hullo!" The plumber, a skinny chap of around fifty, in blue overalls, has arrived early. I take him to the leaking tap in the kitchen. He is calm, doesn't move more than is necessary; his voice is soft and even—the birds hardly seem to notice him at all.

When he comes into the sitting room for a cup of tea, the Great Tits are perched by me.

"They're so tame! They can't be wild birds, surely? Perhaps you've secretly hatched them yourself!" He lifts up his cap a moment and scratches his bald head.

"They know that there's no need to be frightened of me." Tipsy lands on my shoulder but flies off when the plumber moves his arm.

"This is really how it should always be."

"But it's a lot of work." I point at the newspapers protecting the sofa, the curtains that the birds have pecked to shreds, the pock-marks in the piano. "I spend the whole day cleaning."

"Perhaps they needn't live indoors, then, but it's wonderful to see this harmony." He gives the table a little pat, good table, and stands up to get on with his job.

I nod. Still. It's not only that it's so time-consuming: it's impossible not to get attached to individual birds and they don't live very long, as a rule.

Through the window I can see Tinky and Monocle on the bird table together. He goes out of his way to please her, using his whole repertoire of dances, glances, gestures and song. She does pay some attention, but eventually turns away from him. When he flies into her field of vision again, she resolutely flies off in the other direction.

I take the faded red tea towel off the typewriter. Even before I manage to roll the paper into the machine, Baldhead is on the keys. Star comes and perches on my hand. "Come on now, off with you." I gently shake my hand—I don't want to really startle her. Star flies up, then keeps an eye on me from the table. Baldhead briefly flies up too, then lands on exactly the same spot. I click my tongue at him to drive him away before he messes the keys. He gives a little jump, lands on the table, looks at me for a moment with his head cocked, then flies out through the window. Star follows his example.

This latest article tells the story of Baldhead's first mating, with Jane and with Grey. Jane and Grey fought for weeks over the large nest box on the apple tree in the orchard, till they eventually began to build a nest there together, for reasons that weren't clear to me at all. I'd never seen that happen before and would never do so again. Jane's mate had died that winter and Grey had no mate at all. Baldhead, in those days a young and powerful Great Tit, was keen to win Jane and Grey's territory, and their nest box. He courted both ladies, and Baldhead and

Jane became a pair. Jane could sing beautifully, better than many a male—people often think that only males sing well, but that's a prejudice: females also sing, and there is an enormous variation between them. Perhaps that was why Baldhead chose Jane.

Grey didn't forsake the territory, however, and all that summer she followed Jane through the orchard like a shadow. Jane and Baldhead didn't at first appear to find her presence annoying. But when the first eggs were laid, Jane banished Grey from the nest box. Within a few days Grey had built her own nest, in a box not far from Jane's, a very lovely nest woven with coloured threads from my carpets. Baldhead came to visit her in her new nest and for a while the three of them lived in harmony. Baldhead visited both nests while the females were brooding, treating them exactly alike. They used the same mannerisms to beg for food: making little cries, like nestlings, and quivering their wings.

Jane's eggs hatched at the start of May. Now Baldhead completely lost interest in Grey and her nest. A few days later, when Grey's own eggs had also hatched, she eagerly flew to Jane's nest box, where Jane and Baldhead completely ignored her. In the days that followed she increasingly attempted to catch Baldhead's attention, making longer and longer sobbing notes—it sounded like a baby crying. Halfway through May she came back for the first time to fetch cheese from me, and in the days that followed I helped her to feed her nestlings. If she caught sight of Jane or Baldhead she'd call to them. They continued to ignore her. Grey fed her babies alone, and with my help she had more than enough food for them. But she herself hardly ate anything.

A few days later she didn't come to the bird table in the morning. I found her on the ground by the tree where Jane and Baldhead's nest box was. Whenever they flew by with food for their youngsters, she tried to attract their attention. Her cry was so plaintive and her movements so panicky that it upset me to watch her. She seemed to have entirely forgotten her nestlings. That afternoon she died, from exhaustion and sorrow. Her children died a few hours later.

I re-read what I've written. Although most of the reactions to my earlier articles were positive, I also received some critical letters. People think that I've given the birds human characteristics. They don't understand that such characteristics really aren't just human. Birds also quarrel, feel love and experience sorrow. I only write what I see. Perhaps I should take out the words about Grey dying of sorrow and about her panicky movements. Agitated, unusual, extremely intense—there's not a single word that is as panicky as panicky. Is it panicky? I think of the panic that I myself would feel—is panic perhaps too large a word for such a little creature? Yet it does best describe the behaviour I observed. I stand, take a walk round the table. Baldhead comes and perches on the typewriter. "Come on now. Off with you." I take the paper out and drape a tea towel over the machine. "What do you think, Baldhead? Are you thinking anything at all?" He flies out of the window, across the hedge and out of the garden, without a backward glance.

*   *   *

The day after the sixth article has been published, I receive a telephone call from Roger. "Gwen, we'd like to propose something."

Peetur pecks at my sock. I try to shake him off my foot. "Yes?"

"How would you feel about writing a book?" His voice sounds solemn. I twiddle my toes, but that has no effect, so I lift up my foot and give little kicks at the air.

"I don't believe I have the time for that." Teaser lands next to Peetur and hops onto my other foot. Now both of them are pecking—perhaps it's the wool that attracts them. I push them off with my hand. Tomorrow I'll go and buy them some mealworms.

"We'll give you an advance."

I rub one foot against the other—they fly up, then land again. "Off," I say sternly.

"This is your chance to make your research known. It would present birds in a completely different light. And you yourself can choose what to write about."

I push the Great Tits off my foot. This time Teaser stays away, but Peetur is very persistent. "I'll give it some thought." Writing already costs so much time. I really can't see how I could make a whole book about this. On the other hand, I could then go more deeply into their life stories and describe all their relationships. I hang up, push Peetur off my foot. "Come on. Off with you." He startles and I immediately feel guilty. And really there's nothing wrong with him pecking a few threads of wool from that sock. "Come on then," I say to him. He lingers at the window a while. When I sit down at the table with my sketchbook he perches on my foot again, with a very satisfied expression on his face. He picks a thread loose and takes it into his roosting box. He immediately comes back for another one.

And so he contentedly continues. I get hold of my note-book to jot down a few thoughts. Peetur has now set his heart on a red thread at the top of my sock. Birds think by doing, but perhaps that's what we all do.

*   *   *

I re-read the fragments I've written. Not everything is suit-able for a book. But the birds' biographies must definitely be included. And the descriptions of their play, their song, their relationships and encounters. I find my notebooks and all the things I've noted. I don't know how interested people will be in knowing who likes cheese and who doesn't, or how many times a day Star flies in and out. Teaser perches on my hand, then flutters up to my head. It doesn't matter what people want. I have to do justice to their lives and their world.

A soft tap. "Hallo, Gwen." Theo puts his head round the door, then slowly opens it.

"Good morning."

"Have you discovered anything else of interest?" He comes and stands by the table.

"They've asked me to write a book." I point at the chair, but he doesn't sit down.

"Well, that's wonderful!"

"What's the matter?" I try not to sound irritated, even though this is the second time I've been disturbed today.

"Have you seen it?" He's never usually as tentative as this.

"Seen what?"

He puts a newspaper down in front of me. "Bird Woman Lands in Ditchling." Next to the headline there's a cartoon of a witch-like creature with a huge beaky nose, embellished with a couple of warts.

"Is that meant to be me?"

He nods, but daren't look me in the eye. I laugh. "And what do they say about me?"

He laughs too, clearly relieved. "That you're carrying out so-called research but that you have no scientific background and the stories you write are simply invented."

"The first charge is true. I'll never deny that. The second is false and anyone can check the facts." A few weeks ago I was interviewed by a reporter from a bird magazine. I bought cake for him at Theo's. He stayed a long time and bombarded me with questions. I thought he was genuinely interested in my way of life, until I read the article. He wrote that I thought I could converse with birds. I hadn't said that at all. I just said that they often understand my meaning from the tone of my voice, and that they can also learn to recognise words.

"They're attacking that journal too." His voice sounds a little hoarse. Perhaps he hasn't slept well.

"I know where these ideas come from and I believe Roger will put paid to them." I pick up the newspaper and take another look at the drawing. "Quite a good likeness, really." Tinky perches on the piano.

"Do you ever play now?"

I follow his gaze. "Sometimes. The piano oftener than the violin, strangely. They never wanted me to play the piano when I was young, because I wasn't truly proficient. They didn't want to listen to the scales. I could practise the violin in my bedroom, upstairs, and that bothered them less. My sister was a very good piano player." I've heard nothing from Olive for some time now. I keep meaning to write to her. There are always things that take precedence.

"Why did you actually come here?"

Tinky flies up. He always hesitates a moment before taking off.

"If you don't want to talk about it, then of course you don't have to."

Darky, the old male Blackbird who always sings long before sunrise, perches on the windowsill.

"I found the city oppressive. The people." I whistle at Darky. He tilts his head to one side, but then something startles him and he flies out. I also startle a little—I often see what they see.

Theo looks questioningly at me.

I smile. "Would you like a cup of tea?" I walk to the kitchen, where Peetur is perched on the tap. He likes to put his beak in the running water—I don't know if he's drinking or playing, something of both, it seems. I turn on the tap for him.

STAR 13

The Intruder finally left the garden at the end of October, and Monocle lost her interest in tapping—her mate Tinky occupied most of her attention. The greatest nuisance at that time was Drummer, whom I'd so named for good reasons—he hammered away all day long, much to Star's displeasure: she found it too distracting. Perhaps Drummer thought that Star's tapping was her way of communicating with him. He always came when we were busy and would tap on the wood, like Star, but without any kind of structure in his tapping. Once or twice I tried to encourage him to imitate my taps, but he never grasped the intention. One morning Drummer chased Star away, and then Joker took her place. I tapped three times for her, saying "Tap three". I repeated this four times, and then she did give three taps. That was the only time she copied me like that. The following time I tried to tap with her, she swiftly flew into another room.

The next day I called Star, who came to the windowsill. I gave her three taps and then Drummer appeared. He immediately started tapping. Star flew at him and chased him out of the window. Then Drummer came back and drove Star away. It had nothing to do with the peanuts, but was all to do with the tapping and my attention. An hour later Star returned, with Drummer in her wake. Joker also came to the windowsill and started tapping. Drummer chased Joker off, who then went after Star. Then the other Tits grew restless and Drummer flew into the room next door to drive them away.

In the following days Star would arrive very early, so we could tap together before the others appeared. In the course of the morning Drummer would turn up, then Joker would come in the afternoon. But Star watched out for moments when the others were out of sight, keeping a careful lookout for any opportunity.

1952

"Ta-da!" Joseph is holding a package aloft.

"Come in." I put down the bucket of soapy water and wipe my hand on my skirt.

He follows me into the sitting room. "The second impression. After one week." He hands me the parcel, then delves into his bag. First a book emerges, then a pair of socks, and then a bottle of champagne. He puts the bottle on the table and pushes the rest back into the bag.

"Don't you think it's a little early for this?"

"It's never too early for a celebration. Come on, Gwendolen, or may I say Len now?"

He presses the bottle into my hands and comes into the kitchen with me. "I've had another three translation requests: from Germany, the Netherlands and Spain."

"Really?"

He helps himself to a glass and gives me a triumphant look. "Cheers!" He clinks his glass against mine.

"Sshh. Not so loud."

"Well, the birds will gain from this too. Your book is certainly going to make people think. How's the sequel going?" He puts his glass back down on the table. Another rap.

It took me years to write the first book. "Steadily. I'm making notes for it, but the birds demand a lot of time."

"There's no rush. It's just that you've caught people's

attention at the moment, so it would be marvellous if you could have your first draft ready by the end of this year."

"I'll do my best." I don't know if I want to write another book. I have enough material, enough ideas. But it's so difficult to explain properly what I mean. People are so picky, they think the research is pointless, say I'm imagining things. Konrad Lorenz's book, in which he describes how he lives with all kinds of animals, is treated far more seriously than mine, probably because he has proper qualifications, writes scientific articles, is a man. Yet his observations are less original than mine. Moreover, the birds have freely chosen to live with me, whereas Lorenz rears his and so influences their behaviour. The basic principles are utterly different.

Broomstick flies in. He is the only Robin who regularly comes inside the house: last year a pair came twice to take a look; and the second summer I lived here there was a Robin who would often perch on the windowsill. Robins are far more self-sufficient than Great Tits. Perhaps my critics are right—I could simply be making it all up and I don't know for sure whether I'm interpreting everything correctly. I never know for sure. But I also think that other scientists don't know for sure either. In a controlled environment you still have to interpret the facts; you always start out with specific hypotheses. Moreover, even with regard to people, you can't ever really be sure. For example, I don't know what Joseph is thinking now. I think he thinks I'm attractive, but he'll never dare to tell me.

I take a sip of champagne, follow Broomstick with my eyes. Joseph sits down at the table. "Aren't you ever lonely?"

"No. Are you?"

He laughs. "You've got the birds. But don't you ever long for company?"

"Well, you're here now." Birds are excellent housemates. Demanding, but they give a great deal as well.

"You know what I mean."

"That's Broomstick." Broomstick has perched on the handle of my broom. "Robins hardly ever come indoors. He's an exception."

"I can see how he acquired his name." Joseph sits down at the piano and plays a folk song, driving Broomstick off the broom handle again. I sit still and drink. Busby, the cheeky male Blackbird, comes to take a look. Star flies onto the windowsill, then away again.

"I'm very grateful to all of you," I say when he stands. "Especially you. For all your dedication."

"Len, we're awfully pleased with you. And I've got something else here." He puts a bag on the table. "Letters from your readers." He shakes them out of the bag.

"Do I have to read all of those?" I pick up a letter from the pile and open the envelope. It's quite a story, three pages long. "Dear Miss Howard, your marvellous book describes something so familiar to me. I have the sensation that we know each other well, that we're old acquaintances." I return it to its envelope.

"That's up to you."

Tipsy perches on the table, his head cocked, and starts to peck at the envelope. "He's already shredded two letters from the taxman this week."

He laughs. "You're quite something, Len. Listen. There's

a way we could attract even more attention to the book. Interviews. Readings. Could you do something like that?"

"Roger told you to ask me, didn't he?"

"But it *is* a good idea, Len. We only want the best for you. For you and your work." He looks at me pleadingly, crinkling his brown puppy-dog eyes.

"Sorry. That's not something I could do."

"Think it over." He gestures towards the pile of letters, where four Great Tits are now busily pecking. "It could help the birds."

When he leaves I walk part of the way with him. There's a Guinea Fowl in one of the gardens, a living statue. Three of the neighbouring farmhouses have stood empty since the war. They're rebuilding the world now, but not here. Joseph is shivering, in spite of the heat. "Goodness, Gwen, how can you stand it here?"

A field with Greylag Geese. I can smell his jacket beside me, the damp wool, once the coat of another creature. "You're always welcome," I tell him.

On the way back I see our footsteps in the soil, preserved for one night at least.

I sit in the old brown chair by the window until it is dark. The fabric on the armrests is wearing through; the threads beneath are visible, the veins. I haven't seen Monocle for a few days—that often happens, but she's getting older now, and I feel uneasy about it. Birds can simply vanish, in an instant. We always think there's a goal, a reason, that somehow or another everything is for the best, that there's some kind of point. But most lives are little more than an accumulation of chance happenings, moments within the great nothingness.

I walk to the kitchen, past the cardboard boxes where the Great Tits roost—packaging for sugar or grain; people throw such things away when they're perfect for little birds—and I pour myself a glass of champagne. The windows are propped open. The house hasn't yet cooled down. Although the birds were restless, the storm hasn't broken. I wipe the perspiration from my forehead, skin across skin. Slowly the seasons here have lodged inside my body; I move with every-thing that returns: spider's webs in the hedge, frost flowers on the windowpanes, snowdrops, light till the evening's end. Just as once upon a time music also possessed my body. The violin stands in a corner, a relic of a former life. Last year I did go and listen to the orchestra again. Stockdale was as red in the face as ever, but thinner. He seemed smaller. He told me he'd seen my book in a shop somewhere, but didn't ask how I was. I couldn't enjoy the music because suddenly I deeply missed performing. Billie was no longer playing in the orchestra. Nobody knew what she was doing now.

Outside the air feels fresher, driving the heat away. I lay a cushion onto the garden bench. The sky is clear. The news-paper said that there'd be falling stars tonight. I've nothing to wish for, yet I still scan the night sky. I take a sip of cham-pagne, but don't enjoy it.

Clouds pass across the moon, turning the pale white birches into ghosts. In the distance an Owl cries; perhaps it's the Tawny Owl I saw a week ago.

In the morning Star will once again be the first to visit. Her fledglings have flown the nest. She has more free time now and comes to see me more frequently. It's like this each year, and each year it's just a little different. I shouldn't ask myself whether what I'm doing is useful, or whether it's enough. The birds show me that time is not the straight line that humans make of it. Things don't come to an end, they just change form. A feeling becomes a thought, a thought an action, an action a thought, a thought a feeling. The first feeling returns, traces lines through the new one. The first thought sleeps a while, then crops up again later. This is how times intermingle; this is how we exist in different moments all at once.

In bed my heart beats too swiftly. The alcohol traces lines through my body, from my hands to my head to my feet, an unstructured network, nerves. The sheet is cool for only a moment. When sleep comes, I go to the place where memories dwell when we don't think of them.

*   *   *

In late summer Julian Huxley, the biologist, visits me. He wants to ask some questions about my investigation and is curious about my house. He has brought a student with him, a lanky young man with a thin little moustache above his harelip. He makes notes with his fountain pen in a large notebook and rustles the pages so much that in one fell swoop he drives all the Great Tits away. I ignore him until he topples his teacup over the table and even Inkey leaves the room. "If you carry on like this, then they won't come inside again for the next two days," I snap at him. Huxley laughs. "And what are you laughing at?"

"You were just telling me how highly strung the birds are and that you know precisely how to deal with them, that your body knows what to do, that you don't even have to think now about your movements. And here you have a young student who is on his first field trip with me and you don't at all see that it's exactly the same for him."

The young man hunches himself over his notebook.

Yes, but he is a human being. I shrug my shoulders a little. "Perhaps we should go outside a while. It's almost dry. Then I can show you the various nesting places." Outside the noise can dissipate and the birds know where to hide themselves; this is their own terrain, where they have the advantage.

Huxley takes a camera with him, discusses with the young man what he should look out for—he points to the birds, describes their postures, their movements, their vocalisations: that's what they do to strengthen their ties; that's a warning signal; that's what it does to let others know where it is. I guide them through the garden, pointing out the places already described in my book. They encounter a number of Great Tits, the Magpies and the Wood Pigeon who has been living in the oak tree for two weeks now. The Blackbirds don't show themselves.

They're so large. I realise they're unable to move more elegantly, but they could at least try. Huxley has a deep, heavy voice, the young man a shrill one. They talk as if they can't hear themselves, as if they don't understand how much space they take up. As if they can't hear space. We should be able to move noiselessly, like cats; our bodies are soft enough, but we simply don't use them correctly. Joker flies to the window and then back into the garden when she hears the men.

"Do you think your experiment is replicable?" Huxley asks.

"No. Someone could choose to live somewhere remote, like me. They could get to know the birds, build bonds of trust. But the birds would be different. And that's what I was trying to say just now about individual intelligence. I can't generalise, for example, about whether it's the female of a pair who initiates contact or the male, because it depends precisely on who encounters whom and in what kinds of circumstances. It's the same for the nesting place and all the other choices they make. And whether they're introverts or extroverts. There are some universals. Sparrows are bossy creatures. Magpies and Crows prey on the young of smaller birds. But that's more or less it. As far as Great Tits are concerned, I certainly see an enormous amount of individual variation." The young man makes careful notes on everything I say. My attention is drawn to a Magpie in the apple tree, not far from Dusty's nest box—an old petrol can. I stand up. If he comes too close, I'll have to drive him away.

"I'm sorry, would you like us to leave?" Huxley tries to catch my eye.

"No. I'm just keeping an eye on that Magpie." Huxley exchanges a glance with the boy. I don't care. This is my research. My house.

The Magpie flies off. We can go inside again. Someone has pooped on the piano. I go to the kitchen to fetch a dishcloth.

The young man looks at me when I return. I frown.

Huxley leafs through his notes. "Do you think you can actually understand these birds?"

"You don't have to be the same as someone to understand them, although perhaps you do have to resemble one another. But I know what you're driving at: the idea that I'm anthropomorphising the birds. Listen, the fact that Great Tits are members of a different species doesn't mean that we don't have things in common. Darwin wrote long ago that the difference between man and other animals is a question of degree."

"But we can talk with our own species," he counters. The boy gives a nod of agreement from above his notebook.

"They can talk quite as well as we do. With their voices, bodies, movements. Moreover, human language is no guarantee of understanding." Words can gloss things over, cover things up, and long after you've spoken them they suddenly start to lead their own life. "Are you almost done?"

"Last question. Do you still intend to write an academic article about that Great Tit, what was his name again, the one from the counting experiment?"

"Her name is Star. Yes, possibly. Garth asked if I'd like to write an article with him." And there are others who are interested in my work. But opinions always differ about the exact methods to use in order to understand what is going on with birds. They want to measure it. As if feelings were numbers.

"Good idea. It would be a shame to lose all this."

Later I think about that sentence. A shame to lose all this. It won't be lost. It exists between me and the birds, for as long as it lasts, and for some birds that is for the whole of their lives.

*   *   *

"We regret to inform you that we cannot accept your article. Your investigation is extremely original and your writing demonstrates a deep understanding of the Great Tits you have studied. Unfortunately, it is simply too unscientific to be published in *Nature*. If you could replicate the experiment, or better still, enable someone else to replicate it, we would gladly consider such a report."

For a while I remain seated with the letter (no more than ink on paper, pigment on a dead tree). Garth had already said that it probably would not be accepted, even though they've accepted other people's work on Jackdaws and Pigeons. "That's the danger of swimming against the stream," he'd added. "Perhaps, in time, the scientific world will have second thoughts about this."

I had been explaining to him precisely why my way of investigating the Great Tits casts new light on them—because they have to trust you, because they're all individuals with their own preferences and desires, just like us—till he interrupted me.

"Gwen, you know I'm very interested in your work. I think it gives an insight into aspects of bird life that no one else has previously considered. But I can't help you. We could set up a research project together, but it would have to be in a laboratory. Otherwise I'd lose all credibility, and we wouldn't convince the scientific world. You could bring Star with you. We could set up a replica of your house. And there'd be enough time to adapt."

Star would hate it. I've told him that dozens of times. She'd fly off and never return. I can't catch her and put her in a cage. All the trust I've built up with her would vanish in an instant. He did understand that. He understood everything. *Nature* understands it too. Except they don't understand that they don't have the most basic understanding of the matter. You wouldn't put people in a cage, with no company, day after day or week after week, in a strange and sterile environment with shiny walls, smelling of bleach and unknown birds, and then test how intelligent they are. In fact, birds do pretty well in such experiments. It's a wonder they cooperate at all with the petty little tasks they're given, that they don't deliberately dash themselves against the bars, or sit in a corner, refusing to move.

Obviously, I can't make it clear enough to them. I wipe my eyes. How ridiculous to get upset about it. I'm doing this for birds, not for the world of science.

STAR 14

November and December passed in the same way: Star came to the window ledge whenever she could, and she tapped all the numbers from three to eight in response to my spoken instructions. But the number nine still did not work. I tried to practise it with her, but I could not tap it quickly enough.

At the end of January Star began to look for a suitable nest box with Tinky. Tinky had been Monocle's mate, but Monocle had disappeared that spring. She was very old already and I think she died of old age. Tinky was a good choice, at least from the human point of view: he was a much friendlier bird than Inkey or the Intruder, and very beautiful in appearance. As in previous years, Star lost all interest in mathematics: she did come to visit, but her nest and the preparations for her coming brood totally absorbed her. In February she visited only five times.

At the end of March it began to rain. Star came inside more frequently, and that week she correctly tapped out, at first attempt, all the numbers I gave her in words. On 5th April I asked for five, which she tapped in the following rhythm: one-three-one. For that last one, she looked at me a moment, as if in doubt. For the rest of the day she and Tinky were busy with their nest box. The weather was dry, and time was pressing. They had made their nest in one of the new nest boxes on the apple tree. Star immediately permitted Tinky to sleep in the nest box at night. Perhaps she expected this outcome anyway, because of her previous experience with Baldhead and Peetur. Because their nest box was situated behind the house and their territory went beyond my garden, while she was nest-building I sometimes would not see them for half a day. So every afternoon at five o'clock I would go into the garden and call them for a peanut. Star always came immediately, with Tinky in her wake. That afternoon, however, only Tinky flew to me.

1960

"Gwen, there's something I should tell you."

It's still early; snails are slithering across the little terrace in front of the house. Their trails form letters from an unknown language. Theo hands me a newspaper, then takes it back and opens it up. "Here." He points to an article on page three.

"Work on Ditchling Holiday Park Starts This Autumn". I read it again, then examine the diagram that goes with the article. They've bought the land that belonged to the Hendersons and want to use all of it for the holiday park, from the woods up to the boundary of my garden. Where it directly borders my land, there'll be a playground.

"We can't allow this." I hand back the newspaper.

"I'm afraid they've already got permission." He stares at the ground, where a few woollen threads from a sock are scattered.

I fetch my bag. "First we'll visit the District Council. Then we'll talk to those people." I pick up the paper. "Thompson and Co. I'll phone Roger a little later. And Joseph and Garth."

Before we leave, I put food on the bird table: crumbled crusts from the brown bread, butter, some birdseed that needs finishing, three bruised apples cut into pieces. The birds come immediately. Joker flies to my hand first, to say hallo, and only then to the table. I feel a pain grip my belly, then I straighten my back.

We go in Theo's car. At half past eight we're at the District Council offices, in Lewes, but they don't open till nine. It's not worth driving back, so we perch on a new brick wall with trees behind us. Seagulls cry in the distance. We take it in turns to talk away the minutes, till the church clock strikes the hour.

The revolving door jams. I explain the problem at the reception desk. The young woman who serves us—brown lipstick, a white shift dress with green stripes, kohl-lined fish eyes—tells us that we can make an appointment for Thursday. That's in three days' time. "That's too late. I shall stay here until I can speak to someone."

She goes upstairs. Theo drums his fingers on the counter till he sees my raised eyebrows. "Sorry."

The tap of high heels. "Mr Waters will see you at ten o'clock. Would you like a cup of tea?"

I shake my head. "Could I use your telephone?"

"I'm not sure," she says.

"It's very important." I don't wait for her answer but pick up the green phone behind the counter. I dial Roger's number.

"Hallo?" More sleepiness than voice.

"Roger, I'm sorry to ring you so early, but there's a problem. They want to construct a holiday park next to my house. That will mean the end of my research."

He mutters something.

"The playground will be right beside my garden. I'd like you to draw attention to this in your journal, and I wondered if you know any journalists who could publicise the problem. I'd be grateful for any help."

He promises to make some phone calls and says he'll ring me back in the afternoon. I then phone Joseph, tell him what's going on and ask him what I asked Roger. The young woman looks on with a frown. Joseph has less fighting spirit than Roger and fewer connections, but he knows my research well and will do his utmost. When I phone Garth's home number, I don't get an answer, so I phone him at work. His secretary doesn't wish to put me through, until I say that if she doesn't, I'll see that she gets the sack. He also promises to do his best.

"Miss Howard?" A lean man wearing a light-blue suit with slightly flared trousers comes towards us, his hand held out. "I'm Peter Waters. Come this way, please."

We follow him upstairs.

In his office—white walls, wooden table, brown curtains, a tall shelving unit filled with ring binders—I show him the newspaper and point to where I live. "My books have been sold worldwide, in the tens of thousands. Perhaps a hundred thousand copies by now. My first book will soon have its thirtieth reprint. If that holiday park goes ahead, it will mean the end of my research."

"A wonderful book," Mr Waters says. "I'd like to mention that immediately. My wife read it first, then I followed. Our neighbours had recommended it; they thought it was fantastic too. And my mother also enjoyed reading it. I have so much respect for your work, Miss Howard. Perhaps you could give me your autograph? For my wife? I know she'd really appreciate that. We must get round to ordering your second book. I wanted to give it to my wife for our tenth anniversary, but it wasn't in the shops then."

I look at him, expectantly.

"I'm sorry, I'm forgetting why you're here. Holiday park. Yes. I've just checked and all the permissions are in order. The best solution would be to talk things over with the construction firm, perhaps they could leave a strip of land free from development. Or something. I'm afraid there's very little we can do: the land was lawfully acquired and the owner is free to do as he wishes."

"Can I lodge an appeal against the permissions?"

"That's possible. But you won't have much of a chance. It's all perfectly legal." He breaks off his sentence when he sees the expression on my face. "I'll fetch the papers."

When he's out of the room, I look at Theo.

"You should play on his feelings," Theo says. "Give him the autograph he wants, ask him to help you. Play the woman with him."

"Play the woman." I sigh.

Mr Waters enters the room, bearing the forms.

"Mr Waters. I'll happily give you my autograph, and I'm so pleased that you and your wife enjoyed the book. And I'd love to present you with a copy of *Living with Birds*, if you are still unable to order it. But it would be so marvellous if I could continue my research. I'm awfully afraid that all the birds will leave if they start building there." I give him a sorrowful look. "Then it will all have been for nothing."

"That must not happen," says Mr Waters. He draws his shoulders back a little and takes a deep breath. "We'll have to nip it in the bud. At any rate, I'll do everything in my power to ensure that your objections reach the right people."

He helps me fill the form in and adds a note at the bottom of the last page saying that my research is of national importance. He gives me the telephone number of the person who will deal with the case. "This should work." He rubs his hands together.

"Well done," Theo says once we're outside. "I had no idea that such a charming lady was concealed inside you." I give him a dig in the ribs.

At the offices of Thompson and Co. in Burgess Hill we have less success. The secretary makes us wait on a hard purple couch for two hours, then tells us that Mr Thompson won't be free until Friday. I am too tired to quarrel and, as pleasantly as possible, make an appointment for that day.

I am at Theo's place for the rest of the day, making as many posters as I can: "Help Ditchling's Birds—Say No to Thompson's Holiday Park!" Mary offers to help distribute them.

At home I sit down, in the chair by the window overlooking the garden. My feet are sore. I pull off my shoes and massage my toes. Two Great Tits fly to the hedge. My eyesight is too bad now to tell who they are at this distance. Perhaps I've done enough. Perhaps I should finally give in.

Drummer flies to the window, taps his beak twice against the wood of the windowsill and flies swiftly off. I burst out laughing, and then tears fill my eyes. The holiday park can't go ahead, it mustn't. I would have to find another spot and I don't want to leave. I belong here. And anyway, I must protect the birds.

*   *   *

After a number of articles in the local papers, the news is picked up by the *Daily Mail*. The *Guardian* follows with a long interview and photographs of the birds. This leads to me being invited for an interview on the radio. Meanwhile,

Garth and some of his colleagues have sent a letter to the Minister, describing my work as unique and emphasising that the disturbance caused by the construction noise would mean the end of many years of work. In the meantime Roger is busy composing an article about Thompson and Co.'s shady practices, and has discovered that they've also met resistance in other locations. He's convinced that their building methods damage the environment.

On Friday Theo comes with me to the appointment with Thompson. We wait on the same purple couch. Fifteen minutes, twenty minutes, no choice but to wait. After half an hour the secretary brings us to a room that smells of cabbage. Thompson is at his desk, a squat little man with a thin moustache and hands like coal shovels. His shirt collar comes up to his chin. He hardly has a neck at all.

"Miss Howard." He simply nods, does not shake hands. "I understand that you've started a smear campaign against us. I shall therefore be brief. The park will go ahead, and if you create any problems for us, we shall prosecute."

"A smear campaign? I'm simply trying to protect the birds." I cough, attempting to lower the high notes in my voice; deeper voices are always taken more seriously and carry more weight. Take a deep breath.

"We never hurt a fly." He laughs. "Not a fly, not a bird, not a soul. You haven't a leg to stand on. Poor soul."

"Then I'll take it to court." I don't look at him. I don't want him to see my fury.

"I wish you every success."

He sits down, writes something in his notebook. Theo stands and opens the door. "Come on," he says softly. "We're going."

"Do you really think we'll have to take it to court?" I ask as we walk across the square. Pigeons fly up, then land a few feet away.

"I'd wait and see, if I were you. But if we must, we must."

At the shop a familiar figure is waiting. "I just wanted to tell you in person that they're taking your objections very seriously." Mr Waters gives me a smile.

"Would you like to come in?" Theo opens the door.

He looks nervously around him. "Better not. That Thompson is, how should I put it, rather influential."

Theo nods.

"They're going to look again at the permissions. I don't want to create false hopes, it doesn't mean they'll be rescinded. However, they're certainly looking at it." His eyebrows shoot up.

Then he shakes my hand and is off before I can even thank him. "He was acting rather strangely," I say to Theo.

"A nervous chap."

I borrow Theo's bicycle and take a new stack of posters with me. All the nearby villages have been taken care of—now it's Brighton's turn: its public places, cafés, theatres and cinemas.

That night I wake to the sound of a dull, loud bang that makes the house tremble—it must be thunder, but I can't hear any rain. I get out of bed, walk through the darkness to the sitting room, the wooden floor cold and uneven under my bare feet. No storm, no footsteps of a possible burglar, just a gust of wind and two Great Tits who have flown from their roost box in shock and have landed on the edge of the bed. Perhaps the front door has blown open; it's not so robust any more.

I smell it before I see it. Gunpowder. I open the door to the passage. The front door is off its hinges. There's a hole in the wall. I switch on the light, very calmly, and pick up the broom that leans against the doorpost at the back of the passage. It's clear outside, a starrier night than usual. I step into the silence. Everything in front of the house seems in order—the trees stand where they always stood, the picnic table, the garden chairs. I walk down the gravel path. On the wall at the side of the house someone has written in red paint: "THIS IS FOR STARTERS". I put my hand on the bricks for support, their rough edges. Nothing is really wrong, I repeat to myself, the birds are still here, no one is sleeping in the passage.

Inside the house I make tea. My hand trembles as I put the kettle under the tap, and it still trembles when I pour the tea out. I could capture the Great Tits and take them with me, keep them inside till they're used to a new place. I shake my head. I can't do that, they'd hate it. They live here. They're part of the place. They don't belong to me. It would be a crime. And anyway, I've signed a contract for my third book. It's meant to come out this year. A few months back I sent Roger and Joseph the first draft, but they found it too serious. "We want more of those delightful bird stories," Roger said. "This is neither fish nor fowl; it's too anecdotal to convince the scientist, and too serious to appeal to the ordinary reader." Since then the manuscript has stayed on the table, under a tea towel.

On the following day Roger's article about Thompson and Co. is published. It's a long piece—a whole page. He has managed to include details about the attack, and even the television news has something about it.

On Monday morning the postman comes down the path. He had a hip operation last year and doesn't walk well now. "Sorry," he calls from a distance. "I know you don't like this. But I can't get them into the post-box." He points at his bag.

I walk towards him. The bag is full of letters and cards sent from people throughout the whole country. Expressions of support, people offering to help with the campaign.

"Wonderful, eh?" the postman says proudly, as if he is responsible for the content of the post he carries.

"Truly wonderful."

I walk in with the letters—it's a huge pile. Perhaps when they start building we could form a living cordon round the house and garden.

The telephone rings. That'll be Theo. He'll think it's wonderful, too, that so many people are concerned about us. We'll have to organise a demonstration, or a sit-in at the District Council. "Miss Howard, Peter speaking. Peter Waters. I have good news for you. The Council has decided to revoke its permission for the moment, because of possible misconduct on the part of the firm. There'll be an investigation, which could take years, so I assume that Thompson will make the best of a bad job and sell the land. Then the Council could buy it and rent it to you. I'm not saying that this will definitely happen, that would be jumping the gun, and I don't want you to count your chickens before they're hatched. Sorry, I shouldn't have said anything about chicks not hatching. Well, anyway, definitely good news. I just wanted to tell you personally. And by the way, my wife was ever so pleased with the book you signed. Me too, of course." His voice trills with enthusiasm.

After the call I stay at the table for a while, my hands on its cool top. In a moment I'll walk to Theo's to tell him the good news. But first the birds have to hear it.

STAR 15

Tinky was clearly upset. He would not take a peanut from me and flew back to the hedge. I followed him. He flitted back and forth there, calling loudly, and then to the tree and back. I knew immediately that something was wrong. I looked in the hedge, in the tall grasses beside it, in the uncut grass by the trees. Tinky kept fluttering around me. After an hour or so he went into his nest box, utterly exhausted, yet he swiftly came out again, but stayed close to the hedge. I could see no sign of anyone there, nor later that evening either.

The following day Star did not come for her morning nut. She did not come to tap. Nor did she visit the bird table, not even when I was on the bench observing the birds. She did not come at lunchtime, when I had my sandwich, nor later that afternoon when I filled the bird table for the second time. She did not come when I called her and Tinky at the end of the afternoon. Tinky was very agitated that day, spending a long time by the nest box. Once again I stayed outside when the birds went to sleep. It was quiet without their chatter.

The next morning, for the first time in years, I closed the sitting room window.

Two days later I spied the neighbour's ginger cat creeping out of the hedge, near Star and Tinky's nest box. I had no further doubts. He had caught her, at some point when she was flying to or from the nest. For years she had never been away from me for more than a few hours.

Star must have been nine years old when she died. She was at least a year old when, in the spring of 1946, she first flew into my garden. I realised immediately that she was special, although at that time she was still rather fearful. Her talent for mathematics was, of course, extremely unusual; yet just as unusual was the joy she derived from it. Star did not tap for reward, she found it fun to do, fun to work with me. Her understanding was unique; it seemed that she discovered things of her own accord. As if she truly understood me, often before I did so myself.

1973

They keep on knocking. Thief flies past. He's gone before I can turn my head to the window. There is a board by the path: *No Entry*. There's a board by the gate: *No Visitors. Nesting Birds. Please Do Not Go In Front of Bird Cottage*. It's a good job that only Thief was inside. There's a board on the door: *No Knocking*. There's no need for it, no emergencies. There's no one who could have died, it's not wartime; when I go, I'll simply go. There's not a single reason for knocking. I get myself up, stiffer than ever, and peer through a crack in the shutters. It's a young man, green corduroy trousers, a shirt without a jacket, most likely someone from the Council. Or he's here to sell me something or measure something up. I walk back to the table. Thief is back on the windowsill already. Oakleaf comes to take a look. More knocking. I top up the cold tea with some hot. As I take a biscuit, Blackie flies to the table, followed by that little Thiefy. I crumble the last piece of the biscuit, then push the crumbs away with the edge of my hand. Oakleaf has flown out again. There's probably an intruder who needs chasing off. He uses leaves to scare away his enemies. He's the only bird I've ever seen who does this.

Thief is more temperamental than Blackie. He pecks as if his life depends on it. Recently he pecked at my hand when I didn't give him his raisin swiftly enough. Blackie hops from crumb to crumb, in a stately fashion. I hold out a finger and Thief leaps away. Blackie lets me stroke him. Or could something be the matter with Theo? No, Esther would have come then. Or Linda. Or they'd have sent a card. That man is still there. I haven't heard footsteps. Off they go: first Blackie, then Thief, but only when he's sure there's no more food. I lean to one side to pick up the broom. I have to half raise myself. My back. I hold the broom in my hand, then in my other hand, because that wrist has started complaining. I listen for footsteps. Outside Flea and Monocle II and Moses and someone else are calling. I think it must be Donny. I can feel a draught on my leg. I should ask Theo to ring that boy to mend the outside wall. One or two days, that should be enough for the job. But it'll be a disaster for the spiders. Oh, they never watch out for the spiders. Or they say they will, then they don't really try.

Louder knocking. The door creaks. I take a tight hold on the broom, then stand up, noiselessly. He's pushing a note under the door. Then his footsteps disappear into the distance. He could at least try to be quieter. Those notices aren't there for nothing. I sit down again. Meanwhile the tea has gone cold. I close the biscuit tin. Pippa flies to her roosting place, an old cornflakes box above the dresser. In the passage I can hear that there are Crows in the garden, but I don't have to worry about that. There are no nestlings now.

Dear Miss Howard,

My name is Jonathan Brown. I'm a journalist, working for the *Guardian*. I would very much like to interview you about your books and your life with birds. You can contact—

I fold the note in two, then in two again, and push it into my cardigan pocket. I put the broom in the alcove, against the wall. Perhaps he's read my books. Or perhaps someone has commissioned him to do this. Since Joseph died I've heard nothing more from Roger. He must have died too in the meantime. Whether that publishing company still exists or not, I don't know. They haven't sent me *Out of Doors and Countrygoer* for years. It probably doesn't exist any more. Or it's been taken over.

The beans are almost finished. Tomorrow I'll have to go to the village. Saturday, market day, that's good. And I can call on Theo at the same time. He'll probably know what has happened to Roger. Jonathan Brown, never heard of him. Star II flies past me to the sitting room.

You see, Great Tits never stay. At the very most they return.

Before I sit down on the green wooden bench behind the house, I put my cushion on it. They haven't pecked it at all. Neat and tidy they are, these birds, they're all very tidy, there are no more troublemakers now, like Drummer or Joker. I tap on the arm of the bench, three times. Oakleaf is there beside me before I can even see him moving. I give him a nut. Presto II comes and perches next to him. Oakleaf opens his beak, displaying his throat. Presto II recoils. Telling it all again, all over again. No, not all. I can tell him about the birds. They always want to know more. But what? Actually, there's nothing more to tell. Further on, over the meadows, against the hillside, Starlings are twisting and tumbling through the air—a body made of so many bodies, constantly changing form.

*   *   *

A Nightingale. I wake up in a dark room that I don't immediately recognise as my own, remember what my dream was, then forget it. Blackie lands by my head. I sit up, headache, can't lift my hand. Then I can. Blackie flies up. "Good morning," I say to the birds, as I do every morning. Bernie flies swiftly at me, then flutters around. "Come on then." He doesn't give me a kiss.

Thief flits about me as I walk with the plate to the bird table. I bump my foot against the threshold, but I don't stumble since I'm moving so slowly. "Thief," I grumble. "Careful now." They're a threat to life and limb, especially when they're still young. The cobbles are slippery too. I should take the moss off. I must still have one of those scrapers somewhere. In the hall cupboard. Or the kitchen drawer. Blackie takes over. I move even more slowly, step by step across the terrace. I place some pieces of bacon on the edge of the table—here come the others now, Light Brown first, or is it Stripy? The butter, the crumbs of bread, the birdseed. I call Light Brown to me with a nut. He picks a piece of bacon first, eats it in the apple tree. Stripy isn't here. Or is it Light Brown who isn't here? Perhaps I should get my eyes checked again. "Light Brown." Blackie arrives, chases Light Brown off, then Thief returns again. "Come on, boys and girls. No fighting." I go to the wooden bench and sit down. Light Brown lands on my lap. Yes, it is Light Brown. I don't understand how I thought it was Stripy, but where is Stripy then? In the autumn they stay near the house, in the misty garden they know so well. Good birds. But sometimes Baldhead went a-roving. Oh Baldhead, always so bold, always the boss till the very end, till that last spring when he never left my side. Brave little creature. Bronwen vanished in September. Sarah too. "Stripy!" Stripy sometimes listens to his name; at other times he clearly has better things to do. I hold my breath as I call, to keep the sound clear—after a couple of seconds I'm out of breath. I should do some singing exercises. "Jingle!" That dear little Great Tit comes to visit more and more frequently. She was so shy at first. I take a nut from my apron pocket. She lands on my hand to eat it, then flies swiftly off. The other birds come; I can see Stripy too, finally. Blackie has finished eating. I can't see Thief. Over there?

*   *   *

Knock, knock. Creaky knee, getting up is difficult. Tap tap. Dodie is tapping against the lampshade. "Stop it." I flap my hand in her direction, without any result. That thing is full of holes already.

The old wooden floor, slippers, the tiled passage. Fluff.

"Morning, Miss Howard. How are you today?"

"Hmm."

"Better than last week, right? That blinking cold, every-one's caught it." She hangs her coat on the coat rail, with the familiarity of a good friend. "Luckily I've been nabbed by it already." She's wearing a tight dress, very short, too tight for her to move with real freedom. Women are always forced to wear the latest thing that constricts them.

"Quiet, please." Dodie has flitted out already, only Petrus is in his roost. They will come back, though, they know Miranda well enough now, but her voice is so loud and bright.

I sit at the table again. I dreamed last night, for the first time ever, that I could fly. I flew over the yellow autumn fields surrounding Wallington, saw the square where Kingsley and Duds always played marbles, the bench outside the baker's, all untouched by time. I couldn't smell anything at all. Sometimes I smell things when I dream. Cheese. Grass.

"I'll give the floor a quick clean, then the windows and then if we still have time the bathroom, but that could wait till Friday as well." Her voice is less rasping than it used to be. Perhaps she has stopped smoking.

"All right." I've learned not to discuss her plans with her: it just makes things harder and then she says more and more and it takes even longer for her to leave. "Please watch out for the spiders though." A few weeks ago a new couple installed themselves in the corner behind the bookcase. Awfully useful creatures and interesting to watch.

The broom scrapes across the floor. "Won't you think again about getting me to buy a vacuum cleaner for you? They're pretty cheap nowadays. Handy for all those feathers."

I've always managed perfectly well without one. "Would you like a cup of tea?" It's important to keep moving. If I sit too long, then I'll never get up. In the kitchen I put the kettle on. Dark Brown and Light Brown are playing in the hedge. These two little brothers were born this summer and they've stuck to the garden—they sleep in a little box above my bed. Sometimes they come and play on the bed when I've just woken up. Then they slide down my pillow, their feet held stiff, bird skiing. Perhaps they're still here because they hatched late. They were part of Bella's second brood, which she had late in the summer, after her first nest was robbed by that tabby cat who belongs to the new neighbours.

The kettle whistles. Dark Brown is a crazy, creative little bird. He's the only one I've ever seen sunbathing upside down: he hangs from a twig by his claws, his wings spread out—very clever: then the sun can reach the back and the front of his wings at once. But very risky too.

"Cup of tea?" I ask again as I sit down.

Miranda sits opposite me. "They've started building homes in Keymer, for older folk who need a bit more care. Sheltered housing. You can live there independently, but the home is nearby. And you get nursing when you need it. I know you want to live here as long as possible, but they're really marvellous little homes. Light and roomy, with a beautiful large garden. Those Great Tits would like it too, I bet."

Death on a stool in the corner of the room, on a stool in the corner of my head. "I'll stay here." That "here" gouges a line into the air between our faces. Pomfret, the Blackbird, comes through the top window, sees the guest, and twists herself round in the air. She vanishes swifter than she came.

"Your doctor thinks it'd be better if you lived a bit closer to other people." She has a nervous tic, she rubs her fingers across her lips. It seemed to improve for a while, but she's doing it again now. Perhaps she has problems. Everyone has problems these days.

"I have plenty of other people here." Petrus also flies off.

She sighs. "But have you thought about that television?"

I don't know which television she means. "There was a young man at the door recently. A Jonathan Brown. Do you happen to know him?"

She shakes her head. "What was he here for?"

"He wanted to interview me. About living with birds."

"Well that's nice, in't it? A bit of appreciation. You deserve that."

I have no idea if she knows anything at all about my books. "No. It's not possible. It would disrupt everything, drive the Great Tits away. New people make them nervous." I've had quite enough of that.

Miranda takes a sip of tea, then abruptly sets the cup down. "You should do this interview, you know. It's a fantastic chance to get people thinking more about birds. What you said last week, not to peek inside nest boxes 'cos cats can work out where the birds are, no one knows those kinds of things. Even if it saved just one single bird!"

I nod, slowly, sensing the weight of my head, forward, back-ward—brains, blood, bone, cavities, fragile skull. Someone should really take it over, someone young, with true feeling for the Tits and the Blackbirds, with love for them and with a calm demeanour. There's no one. No one has appeared and I'm too busy to look for someone. The days are so short, always growing shorter. I should write things down again. Make time tangible through writing.

Miranda stands up and fetches the mop from the hall cupboard. She goes to the kitchen, fills a bucket. The wooden heels of her sandals always tell me where she is. She has pretty calves.

"Miranda?" My voice sounds shrill.

She pops her head round the corner, holding her face at an angle, as if she's on a photograph, as if she's looking through my eyes at her own face, posing it as favourably as possible.

"Forget the windows, won't you? They'll still be here next summer." All that water. What a waste.

"No, I won't let you face the weekend like this. Anyway, won't it be nice when you can see properly through them again?" A little laugh, her head vanishes.

I clench my fists a moment—release them. There's no point in getting angry. On the table in front of me there's a drawing of Dark Brown and Light Brown. I pick up my eraser. Dark Brown's wing is too long. I'm not sure I can get it right now. An old people's home. Indecent really to start talking about it.

There's a ring at the door again. Miranda opens it before I can protest. It's William Gill of the Sussex Naturalists' Trust, a man with a voice like a tree stump. "Miss Howard."

"Quiet, please," I say. "You've driven them all away."

"We were going to talk again about your estate. So that everything's properly sorted out. Those plots of land you have free lease of too. I've just been to the solicitor's in Lewes and he's proposed this." He winks at Miranda and places a folder of papers on the table. I search for my spectacles.

"Do you want a cup of tea?" Miranda smiles at him.

"No thanks, I've just come for the signature."

Perhaps my spectacles are in the kitchen. I can hear them chattering in the sitting room. It's wonderful that they want to take on Bird Cottage after my death, to create a bird sanctuary. But I simply don't understand why he keeps bringing new contracts for me to sign. The price of land has risen enormously, perhaps that's the reason. My spectacles aren't on the worktop, or on the windowsill. Suddenly the house feels overfull, with all these people. He'll have to return later.

*   *   *

"Miss Howard? This is Josephine Wolch, Dr Stuart's assistant. We have received the results of your tests."

I sweep the crumbs on the table into a little heap with the side of my hand.

"Are you still there?" She speaks too emphatically, as if I'm not quite right in the head.

"Hmm." I brush the pile onto the plate on my lap, then put it on the table.

"Your coagulation factor is too high. But there are excellent medicines for this. We would just like to make an appointment for some follow-ups." I don't recognise her voice.

"What did you say your name was?"

"Josephine. Wolch. I'm Dr Stuart's new assistant. Sandra is on maternity leave."

I thought so. Sandra has a much lower voice, an alto inclining towards a bass, very low for a woman. But beautiful. She also speaks beautifully slowly. This one doesn't. This one prattles.

"I'd like to make an appointment with you for a heart check-up."

Tuesday is a good day. I'm expecting no one then and I can leave the birds alone with a clear conscience.

"How is your wrist now?"

"My wrist is fine, thank you." They kept a tight hold on me, as if I was a child, first the nurse and then the doctor.

They shifted my arm around, asked if it hurt—well, of course it hurt, that was why I'd gone there. I knew it needed some rest, I just didn't know if it had to be in plaster. The steps in the kitchen toppled over. An accident. That can happen to anyone. I held on to a kitchen cupboard with my hand and then twisted it. I still can't play the violin. It doesn't matter. I can take it up again in a few weeks.

When she hangs up, I first put the receiver back, and then find a piece of paper. Tuesday, half past nine, Dr Stuart. I cradle my wrist in my other hand. I can feel that it's hurting now, but I mustn't dwell on that. The plate is on the edge of the table. I stand up and throw the crumbs out through the open window onto the little terrace—Sparrows, a Robin. I can take the bus. That would be best. But then I'll have to leave in good time, because they often come earlier than it says on the timetable. I should go and take a look at what the times actually are. Perhaps I can still cancel it. Yes, it would be better to cancel it. There's no need for a check-up. I feel perfectly well. Sometimes I'm a little short of breath, but that's normal at my age. I'll just have to practise a little with that wrist of mine. Otherwise it'll stiffen up. I don't have to ring immediately. After all, it's next week. Dark Brown and Light Brown skim past me. I should clean the bird table. There was something in the local newspaper last week from the Sussex Ornithological Society saying that many diseases are spread via the feeding places. My birds haven't been ill for years. When I started there were two outbreaks of some disease or other, two consecutive summers. I lost seven Great Tits then. But I don't think it was anything to do with hygiene. It seemed to be some kind of virus, paratyphoid fever, I believe. They didn't all die of it—some of them were just very weak for some time. They had diarrhoea too. And years later there was a whole brood of nestlings that didn't survive. Joker's babies. Perhaps they had pox or a fungal infection. Or mites—the youngsters die of those too.

I go to the kitchen and fill a bucket. White vinegar. I don't know where Miranda has put the sponges.

*   *   *

The blue hour, winter dusk.

The late light gives shape to the leaves, for a little while longer. I gaze until they fade away—their edges seem to be moving. On the windowpane, next to the frame, a drop of water makes a trail, a straight line downwards.

The Great Tits have gone to bed already. I don't put the lights on, stay where I'm seated. My chair was reupholstered last week, I can permit myself that luxury occasionally, and there's a blanket over it now, to keep it in good condition—I might just as well not have had it reupholstered. Someone is moving in the distance, moving the grass—a mouse, perhaps, or a hedgehog. The mice are back. I saw them yesterday.

Theo says I need an assistant, to put my notes in order and send my unpublished stories to that new journal, come on, what was its name again? I showed him my archive of stories, photos and cuttings. He was going to ask the Museum of Art and Craft if they might be interested in them. Theo fell last week, he had to go to casualty. Esther took him.

The garden is dark now—just the window frame catches the light. My face only appears when I stand close to the window and look for openings in the black sky.

I sink back into my chair, close my eyes. Tomorrow I mustn't forget to buy some cheese. They could certainly do with some extra fat for the winter.

STAR 0

The first sun of the year falls through a chink in the curtains. January started seven days ago, and it was grey and dark until now: a new year, but you could not really see it was new. The sun brings colour with it and hope. I go to the kitchen and fill a plate with food for the bird table. The birds have been awake for hours; they rustle, flutter, chatter to each other. Timmy, the little Blackbird, is on the other side of the window, on the sill, his head cocked expectantly. He calls to me, two notes, the same two notes he uses to call his mate. I open the window and put out a piece of apple for him. Baldhead is sitting on the arm of the bench near the bird table, a new little female beside him. I put the pieces of bacon, the cheese and brown bread on the table, then return for some butter, peanuts and fruit. Baldhead comes to take a look. The female flies behind him, takes care to stay out of my way. There is a white patch on her forehead—Star. I suddenly remember that she previously nested in the nest box by the path. Her mate is not with her, perhaps he is dead. She is clearly interested in Baldhead, who neither encourages nor discourages her. Monocle was his mate last year, but I have not caught sight of her for some days now. Baldhead eats placidly, then flies to my shoulder. We both look at Star, who seems hungry and takes a little of everything. But she leaves the cheese alone. After each beakful she looks at us a moment. She is very beautiful. Her feathers gleam and the colours seem deeper than those of other birds. She looks so brightly out of her little eyes. At first she just looks at Baldhead, but then her eyes search for mine. Hallo, I say to her with my eyes. Good to see you. She holds my gaze a moment, then flies off. Baldhead follows her and there they go, higher and higher into the air, ever higher, ever swifter.

LEN HOWARD
© J.M. Simpson

Acknowledgements

I first came across Len Howard's work when I was writing my dissertation for my MA in Philosophy. One of my mother's friends—strangely enough, neither of us can exactly remember who it was; if you're reading this: many thanks!—advised me to read *Birds as Individuals*; shortly afterwards I also read *Living with Birds*. Both books were once bestsellers, but can now only be bought second-hand. Howard's work has largely been forgotten, which is a pity, as her research was well ahead of its time, and her books are still interesting and relevant. Very little is known about her life. In this novel I mix stories from her writings and biographical fact with fiction. Certain passages, such as the sections about Star and a number of the other stories about the birds, have their origin in Howard's own anecdotes in *Birds as Individuals* and *Living with Birds*. The scene at the pond is based on an unpublished story I discovered in her archive in Ditchling, a pale-blue folder containing about twenty different documents and a photo of Olive. Many of the other anecdotes are based on the memories of people living in Ditchling.

I would like to thank the following people for their help while I was writing this novel. John Saunders, the present occupant of Bird Cottage, allowed me to examine Howard's archive and scanned her unpublished stories for me. He told me that Howard left Bird Cottage to the Sussex Naturalists' Trust, which had promised to make it into a bird sanctuary.

The bird sanctuary never materialised, however. Instead the trust sold the house and land for a good price to someone who immediately felled most of the trees in the back garden (only the ancient oak tree is still standing). He also told me that Howard is buried in an unnamed grave, in the graveyard behind her house. Ralph Levy was extremely helpful and hospitable during my stay in his hut in Ditchling. Michael Alford knew Howard and used to see her walking across the fields with birds perched on her head and arms. Eline van den Ende helped me think about the violin music of the period and wrote to me about what it is like to play in an orchestra. Irwan Droog carefully read all the drafts and the final version of this story. Lucette walked into my life while the book was being written and brought light with her. Putih and Olli, as always, have helped the writing process by being with me and enabling me to learn what it is like to share one's life with others.

Pushkin Press

Pushkin Press was founded in 1997, and publishes novels, essays, memoirs, children's books—everything from timeless classics to the urgent and contemporary.

Our books represent exciting, high-quality writing from around the world: we publish some of the twentieth century's most widely acclaimed, brilliant authors such as Stefan Zweig, Marcel Aymé, Teffi, Antal Szerb, Gaito Gazdanov and Yasushi Inoue, as well as compelling and award-winning contemporary writers, including Andrés Neuman, Edith Pearlman, Eka Kurniawan, Ayelet Gundar-Goshen and Chigozie Obioma.

Pushkin Press publishes the world's best stories, to be read and read again. To discover more, visit www.pushkinpress.com.

THE SPECTRE OF ALEXANDER WOLF
GAITO GAZDANOV

'A mesmerising work of literature' Antony Beevor

SUMMER BEFORE THE DARK
VOLKER WEIDERMANN

'For such a slim book to convey with such poignancy the extinction of a generation of "Great Europeans" is a triumph' *Sunday Telegraph*

MESSAGES FROM A LOST WORLD
STEFAN ZWEIG

'At a time of monetary crisis and political disorder... Zweig's celebration of the brotherhood of peoples reminds us that there is another way' *The Nation*

THE EVENINGS
GERARD REVE

'Not only a masterpiece but a cornerstone manqué of modern European literature' Tim Parks, *Guardian*

BINOCULAR VISION

EDITH PEARLMAN

'A genius of the short story' Mark Lawson, *Guardian*

IN THE BEGINNING WAS THE SEA

TOMÁS GONZÁLEZ

'Smoothly intriguing narrative, with its touches of sinister,
Patricia Highsmith-like menace' *Irish Times*

BEWARE OF PITY

STEFAN ZWEIG

'Zweig's fictional masterpiece' *Guardian*

THE ENCOUNTER

PETRU POPESCU

'A book that suggests new ways of looking at the world
and our place within it' *Sunday Telegraph*

WAKE UP, SIR!

JONATHAN AMES

'The novel is extremely funny but it is also sad and
poignant, and almost incredibly clever' *Guardian*

THE WORLD OF YESTERDAY

STEFAN ZWEIG

'*The World of Yesterday* is one of the greatest memoirs of the twentieth
century, as perfect in its evocation of the world Zweig loved, as it is
in its portrayal of how that world was destroyed' David Hare

WAKING LIONS

AYELET GUNDAR-GOSHEN

'A literary thriller that is used as a vehicle to explore big
moral issues. I loved everything about it' *Daily Mail*

FOR A LITTLE WHILE

RICK BASS

'Bass is, hands down, a master of the short form, creating in a few pages
a natural world of mythic proportions' *New York Times Book Review*

JOURNEY BY MOONLIGHT
ANTAL SZERB

'Just divine… makes you imagine the author has had private access to your own soul' Nicholas Lezard, *Guardian*

BEFORE THE FEAST
SAŠA STANIŠIĆ

'Exceptional… cleverly done, and so mesmerising from the off… thought-provoking and energetic' *Big Issue*

A SIMPLE STORY
LEILA GUERRIERO

'An epic of noble proportions… [Guerriero] is a mistress of the telling phrase or the revealing detail' *Spectator*

FORTUNES OF FRANCE
ROBERT MERLE

1 *The Brethren*

2 *City of Wisdom and Blood*

3 *Heretic Dawn*

'Swashbuckling historical fiction' *Guardian*

TRAVELLER OF THE CENTURY
ANDRÉS NEUMAN

'A beautiful, accomplished novel: as ambitious as it is generous, as moving as it is smart' Juan Gabriel Vásquez, *Guardian*

A WORLD GONE MAD
ASTRID LINDGREN

'A remarkable portrait of domestic life in a country maintaining a fragile peace while war raged all around' *New Statesman*

MIRROR, SHOULDER, SIGNAL
DORTHE NORS

'Dorthe Nors is fantastic!' Junot Díaz

RED LOVE: THE STORY OF AN EAST GERMAN FAMILY
MAXIM LEO

'Beautiful and supremely touching… an unbearably poignant description of a world that no longer exists' *Sunday Telegraph*